Dear Tra,

your support!
I hope you will enjoy my
"storeys" (with margarita in hand!)

— Michelle

STORAGE
STOREYS

STORAGE STOREYS

Michelle Black

IGUANA

Copyright © 2022 Michelle Black
Published by Iguana Books
720 Bathurst Street, Suite 410
Toronto, ON M5S 2R4

All rights reserved. No part of this publication may be reproduced, stored in a retrieval system or transmitted, in any form or by any means, electronic, mechanical, recording or otherwise (except brief passages for purposes of review) without the prior permission of the author.

Publisher: Meghan Behse
Editor: Paula Chiarcos
Front cover design: Sam Hlaing

ISBN 978-1-77180-584-1 (paperback)
ISBN 978-1-77180-583-4 (epub)

This is an original print edition of *Storage Storeys*.

Temporarily Talented Terri

(A Cautionary Tale)

It had been hot that day. She remembered standing in line under the blazing sun, waiting for her bus ticket.

"Teresa Rakuster?" The ticket attendant had asked, looking up at her as if he needed confirmation that he'd pronounced it right. Terri could have used online ticketing, but she wanted the chance to say it: "Yep, that's me. Kinda sounds like *rock star*, doesn't it?"

What a relief to be getting the hell outta North Bay! Her stepfather had been coming down harder since her stepbrother had left to work out West. And Mom had gotten muter than ever, melting even further into the wallpaper, the more enraged her husband got. Terri'd always thought it was funny that the expression "keeping mum" meant staying quiet. Her family could have *invented* that!

When she'd been approached by the slender, sharply dressed lady at the rec centre where she worked front desk, she'd immediately known the woman was not from North Bay. At first Terri thought the lady was going to ask her where the washroom was — or for directions to the highway out of town, like most strangers.

"I couldn't help but come over and talk to you." The woman regarded her with a toothy smile. "Has anybody ever told you that you look like Charlize Theron?"

Her face had flushed once she'd realized the lady was talking about *her*. Now she still flushed at the idea of Lorna's approach, but for entirely different reasons.

"I'm sorry?" Terri realized the woman was still talking.

"I said, have you ever considered modelling?"

"Um ... Me? No."

"Well you *should*, honey!" In the same maternal tone that would later be Terri's undoing, she continued: "Say, do you have time for a coffee break? I'd just *love* to tell you about the agency I work with…"

Terri had learned not to trust strangers who came bearing offers so quickly (a rare time her mother had been strong on any point). But Lorna was nothing like the scum around town — she was well dressed; a *woman*; someone who probably had her shit together.

An hour later Terri exited the coffee shop with her, holding some papers in a glossy folder Lorna had proffered midmeeting.

"And to think I'd only come here to pass through on my way back to Toronto!" trilled Lorna. "You go talk to your folks, then text and let me know when I can send someone to get you at the bus station." She said it like it was already a done deal.

Her mom had been pretty easy to convince. *Almost too easy*, Terri thought. She'd given Terri an envelope containing a thick wad of mixed bills "to tide you over until you get your first cheque." She'd kept it as "mad money," scrimped over the years from her household allotment from Terri's stepdad. "Pretty sure this'll do you more good than it will me, girl. Use it wisely, okay?"

Of course stepdaddy was out of the house and out of earshot.

***

Ten days later Terri boarded a Greyhound. From there she'd be brought in an Uber to their rehearsal space "where we have all the new recruits stay until we can match them up with other girls in permanent apartments." They'd driven through the downtown, along the lake. It being night, she noticed the tops of many of the buildings lit up in blue, purple, green … they looked like party rooms or nightclubs. So glamorous!

Lorna assured Terri that she'd have access to the agency's makeup and hair artist. "Most girls starting out in this business have to find their own," Lorna said. "It's good I happened upon you and not some other scout — other agencies'd make you put out way more before you even got to even *see* a stage!"

Lorna's house stylist, Charlie, a trans woman who must have weighed three hundred pounds, pushed out the chair with her foot by way of welcome as Terri entered her room.

"Girrrrlll, I can't wait to get started on those amber eyes of yours!" she'd purred in her gravelly voice, twirling the black chest hair that poked out from her collar.

Terri had also been promised a few pieces of wardrobe. A few days after she arrived, she was invited up to Lorna's suite (*A suite!*). It was the first time since she'd arrived that she'd gotten to talk to Lorna in person.

Lorna threw open the door. "Sweetheart! C'mon in!"

"You get to pick five pieces from my specially curated selection." Lorna motioned toward a rack of glittery, colourful outfits and gowns.

"Five ... really?" She'd never imagined having even *one* of these before. Five!

It hadn't taken long to choose five dresses — they were all so sophisticated (even if, as with all she'd chosen from, they were a bit low-cut).

"Do I need to practise walking out in the one I wear?"

Lorna looked distracted by something out the window. Not turning her head toward Terri, she replied, "No, dear, you'll do just awesome once Charlie's finished with you — oh, and if I were you, I'd start with that little blue number you have in front there." Then Lorna's phone buzzed. "I've got to take this. See you tomorrow night, 'kay?" She waved her hand dismissively before turning toward the window and adopting a markedly different tone: "What is it this time?"

And it had gone on that way the full three days before the first event: Terri would ask one of the other girls how she should prepare and get back vague replies that really told her nothing. It was like she was being patted on the head and sent on her merry way.

"Go enjoy the sauna while you can," suggested Nina, the one girl who'd been friendly toward her. So she did.

Not that she blamed the other girls for their frigid demeanour. They're probably just feeling competitive. After all, there's only one Miss Universe. *And I am the new girl.*

Finally, Saturday came. Terri got a knock on her door at 11:00 a.m.

"Charlie's ready for you." It was Nina, who seemed to have been assigned the role of her keeper for these first days. Terri figured it must be because she had better command of English than most of the other girls.

"Already? But we're not leaving till six."

"Lorna wants you ready early your first day." Then Nina turned and left. But Terri could have sworn she heard her giggle when she'd gotten partway down the hall. Maybe she'd just seen a funny meme on her phone.

Charlie was no more help during their morning makeup session. "Oh, girrrrlll. I've been just *dying* to try some techniques on you. They are just going to *eat you up* tonight!" Then a giggle. Terri noticed her stomach tighten ever so slightly with a familiar discomfort. But her sense of unease started to lift as she watched Charlie work — and by the end, she barely recognized herself. Nothing like the chicks back home.

"Gawd, but you do look like Charlize Theron!"

To please Lorna, she'd chosen the blue dress. When she had more experience, she'd wear the red one and maybe even ask them to play her chosen walkout song, "Firework," by Katy Perry. Tonight, she was just there to watch and learn.

At six on the dot, eight of them piled into Lorna's Escalade and Charlie's Kia Soul. Terri was relieved that the Travelodge where they were staying was not the event venue. When she'd peeked into its one conference room on the way from the pool the night before, she saw it had no chandelier, only pale circles of light on the ceiling from the bottle candles placed on some of the tables.

"The fucking Don Valley parking lot!" Charlie complained when they got stuck in a bottleneck heading north.

Terri also preferred the first highway they'd been on — the same one she'd been on when she got into town. You could see the lake in between all the glass-walled buildings they passed. She was waiting to see if they'd stop at one of those. But almost as soon as they finally hit the exit ramp, they were pulling into the event parking lot. It was twenty minutes north of the city, and the high-rise was more like what she'd imagined, with uniformed valets greeting people in their cars.

But Charlie didn't stop at the entrance. She kept going until they were around back. She clicked the unlock button unceremoniously and gestured toward an entrance. "I'm gonna park. Nina, you know where to go."

Nina led the group to the Maple Ballroom. It was a step up from the Travelodge, for sure. But the space was unnaturally narrow due to a temporary wall someone had set in the middle. And there were very few places to sit — it wasn't theatre style like she expected for a stage show, just a bunch of long tables with a few chairs each on either side of the room, and extra chairs in stacks against the back wall. And no stage! *Are the models going to enter down the middle of the room?* There *was* a chandelier though.

"How are we going to walk out?" Terri said. No one answered; the girls had already fanned out, as if in formation. *Why haven't I been given any instructions?*

Lorna appeared at her right, as though she'd been beamed there. "You ready for your first big night, sweetie?"

"Um … yes of course. But should we not all be backstage or in another room until it's time to make our entrance?"

Lorna looked tickled. "Oh, honey, you *have* made your entrance. And now I'm going to take you around to meet some very important clients."

The other girls were already in full conversation with the people who'd started to arrive, all of whom were men in expensive-looking suits. Terri saw this as a good sign.

These guys probably had connections. She then noticed someone had appeared behind a bar in the back corner.

"But first, drinks!" cooed Lorna, as if reading her mind. "You've earned it, darling."

Terri wasn't sure what she'd done yet to earn anything; and she was surprised that Lorna would want her models under the influence. But she could probably use just one — to loosen up before showtime.

The bar was fully stocked, way more selection than the five basic choices at the Legion back home. Lorna handed her a tall glass of something elegant and blue "to match your dress!" Then she hooked arms with Terri and directed her toward the throng. Terri sipped her blue drink gratefully as Lorna led her to a group of three men who smiled with an avuncular familiarity that comforted Terri. Lorna introduced her as "Tiffany" (which Terri took for an absent-minded slip —Lorna had so much to manage!). One stepped forward, reaching out for Terri's hand. When she extended it to shake, he turned it over and kissed it. Terri flushed. *They must have put a lot of liquor in this drink!*

"Well done, Lorna. You weren't kidding — this new one is something special." He'd said it more to the group, as if she wasn't there.

One of the other men elbowed his neighbour and said something Terri couldn't make out. They both chuckled.

She was starting to feel lightheaded. Through the haze, Lorna was staring at her with an expression she'd not seen before. Clearly, she had put a lot on the line to get Terri here. The room was turning a strange tinge of greenish orange, and the background music swelled up to drown out everything else.

***

Terri was jolted awake by a thud on the wall in the neighbouring room. She was alone, in blackness, in bed but on top of the blankets, naked under a bathrobe… the Travelodge.

Did I pass out? she wondered, panicked. *And then: Oh God, I messed up my first night. What will Lorna say?*

As she got up and padded toward the bathroom, hair matted to her face with sweat and hairspray, her panic morphed into another, more familiar feeling … a fresh ache in her groin area, that gritty sense of shame and foreboding.

She texted Lorna her apology, hoping for an answer that would tell her that no, she hadn't fucked up, and that Lorna wasn't upset with her. She waited a full half hour before her phone vibrated, dreading the reaction she'd get.

Why are you sorry? came back the reply. *You did a really good job for us.*

Terri was still staring at the message when her phone rang. "So how was last night?" Nina asked.

"I think I screwed up," Terri said. "What the hell was in that drink Lorna gave me?"

Nina yawned. "Haven't figured it out yet? We're escorts."

Terri felt her mouth drop, then her stomach again.

"The first night out, they drug us and film us with the clients. Then they threaten to post the film on the internet and tell your family and friends if you try to leave or report them."

Terri gulped, suppressing a bit of vomit that was welling up at the back of her throat.

"But you're lucky. Charlie fucked up last night — ran out of power and the cam didn't record ... I heard Lorna tearing a strip off her."

Lucky! Terri hung up. She didn't have a lot of time. She packed up and took off as fast as she could, landing at a cheap motel on the opposite side of the city. It was one of the few she could find with a vacancy and that she could afford — and the east end allowed her to get as far away as possible from her so-called talent managers, yet still be near Toronto, where a few of her friends had moved to escape their dead-end town.

Over the next week, she did nothing but take showers. In between, she alternated between blowing smoke out the back window and burying herself under the covers, only emerging to pay for another few nights and to greet the food delivery guy. Shades were drawn 24-7.

What is the matter with me? Am I wearing a sign on my forehead: This girl is so stupid, it'll be no problem to get in her pants?

After that first week of running-together days and nights, Terri got up the energy to start contacting her friends. She needed a place to crash. Her "mad money" was dwindling. And she couldn't stomach facing her stepfather, who'd probably have some choice words about how this was what she deserved for thinking she was too good for them.

And what if Lorna's people were calling home, looking for her? What if her mom already knew what she'd been up to?

What if I go to the police? Then I might have to face those horrible people again in court. They probably have lawyers to cover their asses. They'll get off and I'll look like an idiot. And everyone will know...

And so, after following what turned out to be a dead lead to a friend's brother's place, she'd wandered toward the Exhibition grounds, where she found herself leaning against the retired-for-the-season Bandshell, thinking about that day when everything had seemed bright. When she bought the ticket that she thought would start her new life as a model.

What will my mom think? She's gonna know something's wrong. And that it's much more than because I lost a pageant. And what if other people hear about this? In a town like North Bay, bad news travels fast! I'll never be able to show my face again, and everyone will gossip behind my mom's back.

She was roused from her now well-worn mental groove by an advancing sound. A car full of young people — windows and stereo cranked in the still-sultry September air. Their innocent glee made Terri's eyes sting ... but not as much as the song itself: "Firework" by Katy Perry.

Her phone had long died. But Terri remembered spying a phone booth outside the next building over (*Who the fuck uses a payphone anymore?*) and walked toward it; it, too, had seen better days. Gulping hard, she lifted the receiver, remembering recently seeing someone in a movie press 0 for the operator.

"I'd like to make a collect call to North Bay, please..."

Meantime, Terri's sexy evening wear had found its new home: the fourth floor of EZ Storage, only steps from that lake she had so admired.

Nina's Nicked Nightwear

Unit #4231: 6'×12'×8'
This medium-sized unit can be home for all your treasured possessions.

Nina had coveted those dresses since the day Lorna gave them to that new girl. When Nina had started out a couple years ago, they hadn't been forking out nearly as much for wardrobe as they did now. And when Terri had taken off, leaving nothing behind but her first perk of the job and one livid Lorna, Nina knew she'd gotten lucky: First, that chick who threatened her reign as Number One Score was gone (in no small part thanks to her ratting Lorna and company out to the naïve newbie); second, that cunt Lorna was distracted — what with being in damage-control mode, calling *her* boss, reassuring him there'd be no blowback.

"That little girl, she's pretty simple, being from hicktown and falling so quickly for my invitation," Lorna had crowed. "No. We don't need to worry. She may be dense, but she's smart enough to know when to keep her mouth shut. And anyway, we already have people on the inside track. They'll make sure this doesn't touch us. Plus Charlie fucking up the recording means she has no goddamn proof."

After cleaning out the closet in Terri's abandoned suite, Nina had tiptoed down the hallway — thankful that the carpet absorbed the click of her stilettos — holding her breath until the elevator doors closed.

She'd tossed the garment bag in the back of her Jetta and made a beeline to EZ Storage where pieces of her princess bedroom set were now piled and shoved into corners. Among the furniture was her vanity, with its round mirror still attached. Up against one wall was a twin mattress beside a white bookcase-style headboard, atop of which was attached another piece of wood carved into a scroll-like shape with what looked like the dot on an *i* at the top centre, like the tip of a crown. On this board Nina had painted words in ornate violet lettering: *Doubt me. Then watch me.* The same words she would later have tattooed along her wrist.

A hamper of too-small folded-up clothes lay off to one side; the lid, having broken off at the hinges, now leaned up against the wall. A miniature soccer ball had rolled down into the centre where the two clothing piles met. And so here was all her stuff. *For now. Until I stop living out of hotels. Which is what I'm gonna do just as soon as my bank account hits that magic figure and I get the fuck outta the business for good.*

She'd have been thrilled at this point to get another waitressing job — just until she got her esthetician's certificate. Then she'd go back to the CAS and finally get it through their heads that she *was* a good-enough mother. How else had she managed to acquire such a nice place for her little boy to live?

But until that day came, she'd have to stick this out a bit longer. So the day she put the five size 6 dresses into storage (they'd get wrecked in her trunk), she'd also brought with her some little boys' tracksuits and a matching pair of runners. She'd been showing up with new supplies for Ethan — who also wore a size 6, but a child's — for a few months now, every time she got a couple days off and was in the city. Now she could probably get, like, five bills for those dresses, easy.

One of the few good things about Lorna: She dressed her girls well. Served her right. Now Nina would be able to both rip her off *and* gain proceeds from selling the dresses, more that she could put aside to get her son back.

She always made a point to pop in at the office attached to the storage place on her way in. That Ed guy was a fox. Most of the time she only saw his head and shoulders down to his nametag, as he'd deal with her through a window with sliding panes, like the ones they used to have in banks. But a few times she'd run into him in the hall on the fourth and gotten the full view of his tall, ripped frame. He clearly worked out, though she wondered about his confidence. He seemed uncomfortable for such a macho guy, the couple times she'd tried to flirt with him. But that accent! The type of guy she wouldn't even make pay for it. For as long and as many times as he wanted.

Sometimes after she'd dropped off some more little-boy clothes, she'd stroke herself to sleep, fantasizing about the security guard. Now *he* was the type of man that'd be able to help her raise her little Ethan. Someone with a good work ethic, who you'd know better than to mess with!

She thought of this again on her way out this evening, after flirting more than usual with Ed (*How could he miss it this time?*). Swishing down the hall, she turned right toward the elevator, passing unit number 4259 along the way. A few steps before the elevator, she stumbled slightly and glanced down. She'd slipped on what looked like an old hockey card. She thought about taking it for Ethan but couldn't make herself pick it off the dingy cement floor. Instead, she righted herself and put her manicured finger out toward the Down button. With these new dresses, she'd have enough money to buy him a whole whack of new packs anyway. The last time she'd talked to the social worker, Nina was pretty sure she'd said he was into Pokémon cards now.

Marla's Marred Marriage Mound

Unit #4259: 10'×15'×8'
This generous-sized unit holds what you would fit into a four- to five-room home, one you could fill with party guests!

The metal roller door slid up to reveal a scene frozen in time, everything high and haphazardly piled. The style of the contents and dust revealed the age of most of them, not to mention the smell. Yet while some of them matched, the pieces of furniture and boxes of mixed sizes and labels — many without lids — seemed to bear very little relationship to one another.

One conspicuously empty spot along a side wall once housed a dark wooden china cabinet, medieval style, with six doors with keyhole-shaped cut-outs for fitted glass and wrought-iron inserts with curlicued edges that protected the panes. Along the back of the locker, three chairs were stacked, clearly bought to match the cabinet, all wood with black leather cushions; three more were near the doors, two with curved wooden armrests expertly carved at the ends, shaped like lions' claws.

The table that completed the set was also not in the locker (it wouldn't fit), its owner having given it to her youngest, who had wanted a solid-wood table but could only afford particleboard. But the smaller bar cabinet was still there, the same wood as its larger cousin, the china cabinet, but with doors of quilted leather, also black.

When that cabinet went past her the day she watched one or the other of her three children trouping through the hallway destined for the storage unit, Marla had closed her eyes, still able to imagine it decorated for guests, the arrangement of assorted crystal glasses glinting with welcome, ready to serve and to impress.

The rest of the locker's contents held no rhyme nor reason. There was a massive ominous-looking painting of a scowling man in knight's armour against a coal-black background. Marla had always thought it complemented her dining room set. She told everyone the man was supposed to be Don Quixote, but her daughters both went through periods of being afraid of it. She hoped the painting helped more fully express the Spanish style she'd been going for. It matched the specially ordered wrought-iron divider wall they'd had installed — the same pattern as on the china cabinet doors.

That she'd had to leave that behind when she and Harold separated was a sore spot even now, forty-plus years later.

***

Marla got the locker twelve years ago, when she'd needed more space in her mother's basement to store her many eBay purchases and reams of CD cases. It was a weird location, down by the lake, way east of Bayview or Yonge. But her middle child, Rachel, had a connection. Her husband was a cousin of the owners, so they got her a deal. And it was probably because Isaac was such a mensch that the Hurwitzes had never let their employees sell off her stuff when she didn't pay the bill (even though they threatened to every few months — until her brother, John, or one of her daughters straightened things out). Marla figured it was better they talk to them; she'd give them a piece of her mind, treating a woman of her age that way!

The move into her senile mother's home, where her younger sibling still lived, had been her last resort. She'd lost her job as an office administrator not long before her youngest, Helen, had moved in with then-boyfriend Andrew.

It was hard to see her youngest child leave the nest, and Helen's exit had made it harder and harder for Marla to make her rent payments, since she was no longer collecting the few hundred Helen would pay her a month. It also meant the end of her child-support payments from the kids' father. Marla was having no luck finding another office job. Not at *her* age. She was thinking of becoming an Uber driver, but with all the chaos of having to move and put most of her life in storage, Marla simply didn't have the time to even get a resumé done. She didn't begrudge Helen's leaving — after all, Andrew *was* a nice Jewish boy — but without that income, she could barely hold up the rent for the Don Mills apartment. (Thank God she'd been there long enough to benefit from rent control.)

Moving into her mother's meant giving a lot of her treasures to her children, stowing the rest temporarily in a storage unit, then filling her mom's basement with what she most needed. The basement being furnished and no rent to pay and so much time now on her hands, she'd gone on emergency social assistance and discovered eBay and the Shopping Channel. Many of her acquired treasures, a further salve to the wound of loneliness, would take the place of honour next to the piles of photo albums and family mementoes within reach of the double pullout (which in her day had been called a *davenport*). But after a year at her mom's, she'd started needing more space for the vestiges of her former married life. By now, she had a job as a courier, and with a trickle of income finally coming in, so too did her purchases. Every day, it was a changing of the guard of sorts: Marla setting off to take packages to her customers' houses, while other couriers headed toward her mother's house to drop boxes off on the porch.

So she'd gradually added to the contents of the rented locker, hoping that, eventually, she'd be able to use her family's treasured pieces once more; or, appreciating their value, her kids might want to go and pick out what they wanted for *their* homes now. Failing that, she could run her own eBay sale. Now the piles had grown to include photos of her eldest's Bar Mitzvah; first finger paintings from all three kids; the English bone china; her Villeroy and Boch dinnerware set, complete with serving bowls and gravy boat (and the fish knives that had come from a lower-tier company but matched them so well with their carved bone handles); and Royal Doulton figurines. And then there were the collectible items: her Barry Manilow and Sinatra albums, still mint (even if she didn't know which boxes they'd ended up in — the movers had been so careless). In any case, her storage unit was a veritable treasure trove! She could not — no, *would* not — part with any of these items, they so recalled better days — days she could be proud of.

And days her children would no doubt want to recreate once they started to grow their *own* families. Though she'd been sad to hear the words "junk" and "garbage" under their breaths as they blew past her coming on and off the elevator, in and out of the hallway, carting more of her things to the locker. It had taken several trips — her unit was at the very end of the hallway.

And she'd tried to keep things intact. Made her payments for the locker with her much-reduced salary. Then her mother and brother had pitched in for a few months — it'd only been about $250 back then. But now she was simply unable to make the payments and still have the life she was entitled to after spending most of her life giving everything to her family. Which had become another of the many issues and arguments between her three now-married kids, all of whom had been called upon more than once to pitch in a payment or two for the unit. After all, whenever they were ready, all of it could be theirs.

They just have to agree on who wants what. All the memories in those boxes ... their school pictures, artwork they could show their own children some day...

"They just have to say the word and they can come take. But instead all they do is argue about who's going to pay," she would wail to her neighbour in the shared parking lot of her mother's townhouse.

The one thing her kids did seem to agree on? That she should just get rid of most of what was in there. Her middle daughter had even called her a "hoarder." Marla took great issue with being characterized that way — and by her *own* child. So she'd filled her basement room with years' worth of eBay finds. It was amazing what you could get these days without ever having to leave your house. And the CDs, well ... wasn't the experience of music something everyone deserved?

That things had gotten to this point was all Harold's fault. When she had asked, her husband had provided. And she'd gotten used to trucks pulling into their three-car driveway, bearing more furnishings and décor.

She'd been proud to flaunt their lifestyle to the neighbours. He'd worked most nights while she raised their three children. And being the one with more daily contact meant she could raise them the way *she* preferred — to be creative and spirited, like her (and always immaculately dressed).

After being in their starter home for three years, they had Stephen. Then they moved up to a house twice as large and with a much deeper yard. More space for her little cherubs! But more to clean too, so they'd picked up a nice Russian girl along the way, who not only cleaned their house but also provided babysitting in an emergency — like when she needed to shop for a new outfit for one of Harold's work functions. They'd always been able to enjoy the best of the best — even though Marla would still find fault with how Ludmila seemed to leave several parts of their bathroom out of her cleaning repertoire.

When Harold's last support payment had come in, Marla had wondered, *Why should now be any different? Shouldn't he keep paying to keep up her current — though much scaled-down — lifestyle?* She was pretty sure Harold's new paramour was behind his decision to cut her off completely. For all his faults, Harold wouldn't have decided on his own to stop helping her — she *was* still the mother of his children, after all! And Marla knew he was still giving money to Rachel, now that Isaac had been downsized. And it was the least he could do, to keep helping her, after she'd endured the stress of being married to him and raising his offspring; she was of the theory that this was why she'd been dismissed from her last good job at the ministry too. The post-traumatic stress sometimes still got to her. More than once it had interfered with her being able to stay on track with her work. (She was only half-convinced that her humiliating dismissal had been due to *redundancy*.)

All these years later, she still questioned why she had married Harold without ever really loving him. She was pretty certain he had never loved her either — it was hard to know whether he'd even *liked* her, near the end. They were just in the same place at the optimal time for mating: she in her early twenties, he a bit older and already established as a realtor after a brief stint as a car salesman. He was athletic and strong, his demeanour composed and measured, not prone to rash outbursts or decisions (or not back then, anyway).

And, of course, he was Jewish, which made it much easier to convince her parents that he was the right choice. And like hers, his family was Reform: just devoted enough to observe the more conventional traditions — Rosh Hashanah always meant a catered dinner, and Chanukah had been a wonderful time for the kids when they were young — but not so much that they'd have to spend much time in shul. Other than when their son had been preparing for his Bar Mitzvah, of course. By the time it would have been Rachel's turn to decide whether she wanted a Bat Mitzvah, Marla and Harold's foundation was well into crumbling; so there would be not nearly as much effort devoted to giving their girls the same as their brother had enjoyed.

All in all, Harold had seemed like a good match, as good as any she'd met. And she was so ready to leave her parents' house. (Her mother had never been particularly warm and had been hypercritical of Marla long before senility and then Alzheimer's had set in.)

But add ten years and three kids, and she started to see nothing but the cracks in Harold's armour. And his anger. No longer the mild-mannered man she thought she'd married, Harold would yell loud enough at her sometimes that the kids could hear it from two storeys up. Usually, it was in response to her requests that he deposit a little extra into her household spending account. Kids — and the new house in North York — didn't come cheap. And they had a reputation to maintain!

***

Marla thought it was worth it to pay the extra fifty bucks a month for the high-floor unit, which now housed the fruits of all those commission cheques: Her things were in the newer building, the climate-controlled room. And the building was still so new and clean. The girl in the office had told her when she'd first toured the facility, "The floor is so smooth and new here, if you were a skateboarder, you'd *love* it!" It was of a standard befitting her most precious memories of her children's formative years.

That's why she didn't at all understand their acrimony toward the storage unit. So what if they'd had to pay for it once in a while? It was their treasured memories she was holding onto! One day they would come for these things and be *thankful* to her for having put them in a safe place, until they were in bigger houses and could properly accommodate (and maybe even display) some of her valuable acquisitions. Take the silver they'd gotten for their wedding — she was sure Helen would want that.

Her youngest had always had the best taste of the three; she could only hope that Stephen would have married someone with the same taste, who might want the bar set — or at least its contents, all those different glasses that had added elegance to the many, many evenings they'd entertained Harold's associates, when the kids were still babies. Those glasses held all kinds of cocktails over the years: gimlets and daiquiris in their Waterford Cocktail Essentials collection; plain old rum and coke or straight scotch in the bowlers. Now all those pieces had been rolled in paper and stuffed — *Probably sideways*, Marla thought — into three cardboard boxes.

Stephen's wife, Laurel, had been the one to pack up their glassware. Which figured. Marla frowned. Typical of a gentile, she had turned out to be not at all the domestic type. Even so, if you had to ask her right now whether she liked her son or her daughter-in-law better, Marla would probably hesitate before answering. At least Laurel demonstrated a modicum of decency in how she addressed Marla, in a way that conveyed the respect that she was entitled to as the family matriarch. Though he'd always be her number-one son, when it came to his attitude toward his mother, Stephen was a whole other story. He had unfortunately inherited his father's quick-to-anger character flaw.

Marla had been so grateful when that very polite security guard who watched over EZ Storage had stepped in on yet another argument started by her son — though the man hadn't work there then. That day, the argument with Stephen was outside the rental unit offices where who *knows* what kind of people frequent. Thinking back, Marla wondered if she'd had anything to do with getting that nice young security guard the job. He looked a little rough — not as refined as her Stephen — but he'd behaved admirably in defending her.

It was hardly the first situation where Stephen had lost his temper like that with her, nor the first time in public. But it was especially embarrassing and painful to have this happen at the site that held the last vestiges of her family, from the time when they still had a family that was the envy of their neighbours.

Only a year or so after Stephen had started seeing Laurel, Marla, after another such humiliation by her enraged son, shared with Laurel how distressing her ex-husband's anger had been to her. She preferred to put the focus on Harold again, rather than interfere with the longest relationship her son had managed to have to that point. And it gave her a more neutral party to talk to about her many trials. She'd used the opportunity to both regale Laurel with a memory and recall her former high-end serving pieces.

"You know, there were times I got *so* mad at Stephen's father. I would pick up a dish to throw at him and then realize, *I'm about to break the Royal Doulton.* So I stopped myself, realizing I couldn't stoop *that* low."

She'd kept the Doulton but left the husband — that was her intended message to Laurel. She wouldn't dream of raising the subject of her son's anger to his new girlfriend, not then, anyway. Even if he could be just *abominable.* And now, rescued from Stephen's tyranny and Laurel's slackness, the Doulton lay wrapped in newspaper, in one of the boxes that had a lid.

Lately, her kids all seemed to be fighting with each other — sometimes one pair or another would fight with each other, and the third would always call to complain to her about the other two, a pattern that had persisted for decades. More recently, their feuds seemed to mostly be over payments for "the locker." But they'd managed to come to an agreement on *something*: her youngest, who must have drawn the shorter straw, had just invited her for lunch, during which, spreading cream cheese on a bagel, she had informed her that the locker and all its contents would have to go.

Stephen had been first to raise the idea that the time had come. Yet he'd refused to have anything to do with the move. He felt he'd paid enough for all that junk, and his sisters probably had more use for it than he did. The only things he wanted were his albums of collectible hockey cards, which he was sure were in a box somewhere in that maelstrom of crap.

So when Rachel and Isaac and Helen and Andrew would meet up at the loading dock with the strapping young Junk-It employees the third Saturday of next month, Stephen instructed them to put aside two old file boxes with no lids. There'd be a pickup of donations for the Diabetes Association as well. (Marla knew that this little philanthropic touch would be the handiwork of her bleeding-heart daughter-in-law.)

"The only thing I want from that shitwreck are my hockey cards, if you can find them under all that useless crap," Helen quoted him to Marla.

He shouldn't have to go all the way there just for *that,* he'd whined when he called to confirm that he had been part of the conspiracy against her, yet to a much lesser degree. The whole affair was causing Marla no small amount of anxiety. She marked each day in her pocket calendar from the time they'd announced their decision to dispose of her things. (Who needed a "smart" phone, when you could write on paper without having to remember a password?)

With Junk-It hired, she feared they would likely keep very little of what she'd been preserving for them. And with her already high blood pressure, and as broke as she was, not to mention that there was still no space for all her treasures where she lived — who knew how much of it was going to end up donated, with sets broken up into items sold piece by piece in some second-hand shop? And how much of it would not even be spared its dignity to that degree? What would bypass the donation truck and be deemed junk, tossed in the trash, never to be appreciated again?

The final question she didn't yet know the answer to — and the most insistent: Once the locker's contents were no longer hers, who — *what* — would she be then?

This was the thought that had distracted Marla on her last drive down Coxwell before the kids would make their final visit. *She* was going to be the one to save Stephen's beloved hockey card collection. Maybe then he would start to treat her better. And she'd take a few things that had meant the most to her girls too: their first dresses, their Dr. Seuss collection.

Marla locked the padlock for the final time, the haphazardly packed file boxes in her arms. As she turned, the elevator stopped to let in another renter. As if sucked by the draft as the elevator closed, out flew an escapee from Stephen's hockey card album: a 1964 Yvan Cournoyer rookie card, unseen by Marla, who barely nodded at the other renter as she carried her treasures onto the elevator and waited for the doors to close.

Walter and Mary's Wardrobe Malfunction

Unit #3123: 6'×12'×8'
This compact unit holds all the finery you could fit into a walk-in closet.

Walking into unit 3123, a person might think they were entering a fashion warehouse clearance sale. The first thing they'd notice would be how *organized* everything was. Along all three walls, with the middle part leaving enough width for a person to stand with arms akimbo, lived rows and rows of wardrobe racks, all full of women's clothes neatly arranged on hangers, a stream of colourful fabrics. There were many of the exact same items in three or more colours arranged next to each other, as if inviting a shopper to choose. The only thing that belied the possibility of a retail environment was that every single item was a size 8.

Melody had chosen the fuchsia blouse the night she got hit by that car.

They'd been out at a work friend's end-of-summer party — a backyard do — and Melody had gotten a new 'do of her own, a rare upsweep of her usually untamed locks. She'd also chosen to wear a skirt that she'd had *before* Walter started bringing her clothes. (She'd laughingly said he was "styling her.")

Walter remembered pushing that incessant thought out of his head when they'd been getting ready to go out. It didn't have to mean anything that the unlikely turn Melody had taken, in her uncharacteristic choice of hairstyle, foreshadowed other, more life-changing turns to come. Like when she'd run out into the road laughing, with the aim to admire an abundant garden on the opposite side.

But Walter would still kick himself for not suggesting she pair the fuchsia cami with one of the matching skirts he'd given her.

Walter was in tax accounting, a career he'd inherited from his dad, who had emigrated from Eastern Europe (though, as rumour among some circles had it, Romania had not been his birthplace — that had been Israel). But Walter didn't ever uncover definitive evidence of that, so he felt it better to dismiss it outright. Much easier to sleep at night, without anti-Semitism to contend with.

Walter had always had a secret longing to be in the fashion business. Not furs, which his cousins had made a killing with; more the array of clothes women could wear for work and the even more bewitching range of styles they could put on for night.

So when he met Melody, it had been Walter's chance not to be cut from the exact drab shade of beige cloth that his father had been. She LOVED to wear colours; it had been in her dating website profile — complete with the all caps.

He still smiled wistfully thinking of Melody repeating those sentiments gleefully when they'd had their second date and were bidding each other good night — her proclamations about the things she liked and the things she didn't were so pure. "Things That Are a Royal Pain in My A$$" — that had been the name of her blog for a while. Tasteful, PG-rated use of dollar signs in the title and all.

From what Walter could now recollect — it had been such a life-before-your-eyes event for him. *So traumatic*, his sister would later say — it must have started as a good day for Melody, for her to have broken out the fuchsia. Yet still, there'd been that old grey skirt she'd worn with it. He would never have given her that.

So wasn't it just the thing that, in the end, her love for bright colours had made her dash into the street like that?

***

He'd not been with Melody long enough for them to start a family. So now, left entirely to his own devices, Walter started spending a few evenings a week in the "Bucky's" near his office, working into the night to salve the wound of the enormous loss. Starbucks had a grating yet not unwelcome effect on his ability to set a routine and stick with it. It was one of the things that had made him such a success in the industry: the old-style stick-to-itiveness that Walter embodied. That would be the difference between surviving the Internet Age and being usurped by a bunch of damned delivery drones to feed the Amazonian appetites of every consumer with a keyboard. And he could have a fair-trade, organically grown, thinking-man's cuppa joe. More important, the coffee shop was located almost exactly between his office and the nearby storage unit where he still kept his dead wife's clothes.

And thus it was at Starbucks that Mary fell backward into Walter. He'd put his arms out to catch a fuchsia wool three-quarter-length coat containing Mary. It wasn't the typical romantic *meet cute*, the new term he'd read about. Not in a *When Harry Met Sally...* way, nor even a cheap rendition of the lobster kitchen scene in *Annie Hall*. It had settled — like many things he would come to feel about Mary — for being just awkward. Not dangerous or life-threatening. And in that, also comfortingly harmless.

But still. It had been one of the more interesting and colourful things that happened to Walter in the eighteen months since he had decanted Melody's ashes and found a spot on his living room mantle for the empty urn. And there was that flash of fuchsia to give Walter pause, then reflexive action.

Mary had breathlessly said, "Did I spill your coffee? Are you okay?"

Walter had thought it so refreshing that this tiny woman who'd escaped cracking her head on the hard floor of the coffee shop was worrying about how six-foot-tall, 250-pound Walter was. He'd offered to buy her another coffee to replace the one that now lay spilt where she'd have landed had he not intervened.

They'd ended up staying there together for another two hours. Two hours that could have been minutes — or days. Walter didn't notice. Mary enthralled him from the moment he went to get a chair so they could share the tiny round table he'd plopped his laptop onto (his regular space — this was one of the more off-the-beaten-path Starbucks, so he'd managed to secure a spot that over time became his).

It wasn't anything specific she said that made him so taken with her — though he had managed to learn a lot about her in that first meeting: Left at the altar a few years earlier, Mary had since lived alone in a condo with her two cats; she managed a flower shop around the corner from the coffee shop.

And she just loved books, being the organizer of a book club that met biweekly, its members rotating houses every second Sunday. Mary was also an avid follower of French cinema, especially the old stuff. "From the great directors in the WWII era — you know, Jean Renoir, François Truffaut, René Clair, Robert Bresson…" She didn't speak French, which became obvious as soon as she'd started proudly rhyming off the directors' names.

"There's just something about the way everyone looks and dresses in those films," she said. "They just take so much more care with how they put themselves together. It's like they want to be a work of art too."

Mary looked as one might imagine: usually in a tastefully snug calf-length pencil skirt and a cap-sleeved blouse in pale shades ranging from pink to dove grey. The fuchsia coat she'd worn when they'd first collided was the most stand-out frock she owned. Walter was surprised by how at home he already felt with her. And he couldn't help noticing, she was a perfect size 8.

So after that first meeting, Walter made it his goal to pluck Mary from her single life, like one would pick a daisy from a savage field of weeds, and gently and gradually tend to this new bloom. He was surprised at his sudden readiness to start dating again. Up to that day, not one time had he thought about moving on from his duty to uphold Melody's memory. He didn't feel even close to being done grieving for her. But Mary had a quality that immediately drew Walter in; she just seemed so *safe.*

It was as if, being quite at the other extreme from Melody's personality, Mary was unlikely to leave him like his wife had. He was only mildly conscious of the anger he still felt at the way Melody had been lost to him — had she not been so flighty and excitable, she would no doubt have seen that car coming. *And she would have gotten the hell out of the way in time.*

But another way he found to salve the still-gaping wound was his weekly ritual of visiting the storage unit. Every Sunday afternoon, once he'd finished his weekend chores and errands, Walter would make his way to unit 3123 and, with an air of solemn reverence, roll up the door and find his senses flooded by the three burgeoning racks of vibrantly coloured, indulgently textured garments that lined the walls. To him, this gesture was far more appropriate and meaningful than visiting her gravestone — especially in winter. It felt more like entering a garden.

And it came complete with a hint of woody floral — her signature fragrance, Samsara by Guerlain. "*Le français, bien sûr!*" Melody would lilt, her accent authentically French. Most of her clothes still carried a hint of the perfume, though there were several pieces that had never graced her form, still with the original store tags. It didn't matter to Walter. She had somehow touched them all. And in many cases, he had too.

Like a retail employee performing exacting inventory, Walter would lovingly thumb through the racks, at times stopping to pull a garment toward his face and inhale deeply, then carefully sliding it back into its space. He'd arranged everything by season. And the pièce de résistance? Walter had also assembled pieces that he remembered Melody wearing as outfits.

And he would continue with this ritual as he got to know Mary. Over the seven months he courted her and as she started to return his affections, Walter would continue his twenty-minute pilgrimage south down Broadview, then straight east along Eastern to Coxwell. With Mary at her book club every other Sunday, Walter had been able to keep his regular appointment without fail. While she had started staying at his place most weekends, she still needed to be home to feed her cats again, so she'd usually say her goodbyes midday Sunday, then head to either her book club meeting or home for the night. She usually had an early delivery of fresh posies to unpack on Mondays.

By this point Mary had started to ask the odd question or drop the odd hint about whether Walter would ever want to take things to the next stage. She was too traditional to cohabit — even with the sleepovers, it would still have to be straight to engagement for her. And with them both being in their late thirties, it stood to reason that she was starting to get impatient for discussions of her desire for a family.

And Mary was very respectful of Walter's need to continue holding homage for Melody. She didn't ask him whether he was still pining, even though there were pictures of his dead wife around Walter's place (where they spent most of their time), and of course the urn that never left the mantle. Even when Walter mentioned once or twice that he still thought about Melody every day, she'd nodded, her smile unchanging, and patted his arm. Walter tried to keep his grief mostly to himself — he didn't want his new love to think his mind was ever anywhere but squarely on her.

And so their relationship went on, Mary turning out to be just the type of mate Walter now needed: After the unpredictability of vivacious Melody — *right up to the way she ended her life*, Walter would think later — Mary was a more muted shade of fuchsia, in a more practical fabric; she was docile and malleable enough to keep Walter content yet bore just enough resemblance to Walter's first love that she still inspired a sense of the forbidden in him.

***

After a few months of dating, Walter began giving Mary surprise gifts of clothing.

"Silk in emerald green? Oh, *thank* you! I can't wait to try it on!"

Then two weeks later…

"Oh, Walter, how did you know I would like this dress? It's like you can read my mind!"

Then after another two weeks…

"Oh myyyyy. Walllll-ter. This is amazing! Two different colours of the same beautiful sweater?" Mary was now experimenting with styles and colours she would normally not consider, but which she knew would please Walter.

And on it went, with the fashion choices changing with the seasons.

So it was in a pair of black Lycra palazzo pants that Mary arrived at Walter's place on a Sunday in early

October. She'd done some cleaning up at the shop that weekend and hadn't seen him since the previous week, so she was eager to surprise him — and disappointed when she found his driveway empty. This had happened twice before; the other times he had muttered something unintelligible, and she'd thought it best not to push the issue.

This time something felt wrong. She decided it was time to probe.

"Ummm, Walter ... I was wondering, where were you earlier this afternoon? I was thinking of dropping by but drove past and saw no car."

"Oh. Really? Oh. Sorry. I-I was at the office."

"On a Sunday?"

Walter looked at the floor. Then back up at Mary. "Yes, I find I get more done sometimes going in on the weekends, when there's no chance anyone will call or walk in. You should have texted me. If you ever want to get together, well, you know I'll make time for you, darling."

Mary frowned. *Why do I feel like he just verbally patted me on the head and sent me on my merry way?*

But then, being an accountant, Walter wasn't much for surprises. Especially after life had surprised him enough by sending that car hurtling into the first love of his life.

The only time she'd felt any particular concern about their relationship had been when he surprised her on one of their Friday dinner dates with a coat. Walter had found one in his locker that Melody had worn only a handful of times. But he'd proffered it only a few days after bringing her a new skirt.

Walter had explained that, rather than buying her jewellery (she only wore her omnipresent cross and the odd pair of pearl studs), he thought clothing was the best type of personal gift. Wasn't it a loving expression of his admiration for her beauty? Didn't she tell him about her customers at the flower shop who'd complained that their clueless partners had gifted them with appliances and tech gadgets?

She'd nodded and smiled brightly up at him (they were almost half a foot's difference in height), as was her regular way when she was agreeing with what he said. Which — one thing Walter almost appreciated in her more than in Melody — was pretty much all the time. And when she *did* find herself disagreeing, it was about benign matters, like what music she was in the mood for or where they were going to have dinner. Most of the time, Mary was a like a bobblehead, nodding at Walter's every utterance.

It would turn out that Walter had underestimated just how much Mary really was paying attention.

Walter had gotten comfortable in his Sunday routine of visiting his "hangar of hangers," as he'd come to cheerfully deem it in his mind while pulling out of the driveway, his course set toward EZ Storage. The initial few remorseful pangs he'd felt in those first months with Mary had almost evaporated now that he had the dual mission of both honouring his former wife and gifting his new love. He'd wrestled with what to even call those pangs when they'd gripped his throat on the first few Sundays after Mary'd left for book club.

What was it he felt? Not exactly *guilt*, certainly not at the beginning, when he hadn't known Mary long enough to wonder if visiting his dead wife's wardrobe might represent any sort of betrayal. They were the prodding pangs of that feeling of needing to keep himself more guarded. Because in Mary he'd finally let someone else close enough who might possibly have something to say about how he spent his Sundays "at the office."

And it was this lightening of his spirit that would betray Walter.

Because while Mary seemed to agreeably absorb all that Walter said, with her open, receptive expression, without question or suspicion, she was always listening carefully. And just as importantly, she noticed inconsistencies. And what she couldn't match up in her mind were the many, many times that Walter had told her about how unhappy his job was making him. So when he jauntily walked her to the door before leaving "for work" — *on a Sunday afternoon* — she couldn't shake the discomfort she was feeling.

"Walter may be an accountant, but something here just doesn't add up."

When it came to where he was spending every Sunday, Mary was no longer prepared to accept the story without reservation.

***

Sometimes it seems like Walter feels superior to me, like I'm his niece being sent off to play after tugging on his suit jacket to ask a question. But on the whole, he really has been indulgent. And I'm happy ... well, content, anyway...

But if there's one thing I don't cotton to, it's being lied to. Why is he so determined to go to the office on Sunday afternoons? Even on those weeks I had no book club? And last Sunday, I wanted to take a stroll in the autumn leaves, and he wouldn't waver from his routine. I knew being with an accountant would mean certain things would be predictable. But not like this...

What's really started to niggle at me lately is the perfume. All those clothes he brings me. Even removes the tags and washes everything first — but why do so many of them smell like Samsara?

My accent may be weak, but I'm a serious Francophile. I know that scent from Maison Guerlain ... always found it too prétentieux. *Samsara — didn't one of my novels say it means the cycle of death and rebirth to which life in the material world is bound?*

At first I thought maybe someone in the store had tried it on and the smell had lingered. But practically everything he gives me smells like Samsara. And that one Sunday when I surprised him after book club ... it was all over him. Is he keeping another woman on the side?

These were the jumble of thoughts that almost made Mary miss her left turn as she tailed Walter at three thirty on that chilly Sunday afternoon.

***

Mary's chest sank as she made the turn onto Eastern Avenue, having by now bypassed the Beaches and his office. *This doesn't look like an area with accounting offices. He* is *going to see another woman!*

They drove for ten more minutes through the industrial area, all film studios and gritty auto-repair shops.

"This isn't Walter's scene. I might be right," she muttered. Her mood started to plummet further. Mary didn't drive much anymore, what with Walter having the nicer car and preferring to take the wheel. "To give you a break so you can just enjoy the ride," he said. So she had to focus extra hard on the road, her mental state being a dangerous distraction.

"It's bad enough that he's mumbled Melody's name some nights. Okay. *That* I can handle." It was one of the things that she loved about him — how loyal he was to his former spouse. "And it's not his fault what happened…" Mary continued talking to herself as she kept her eyes on Walter's Lexus, all the way to a parking lot, where he turned in.

EZ Storage? I don't remember him mentioning a storage unit.

She had slowed to a crawl so he wouldn't see her. Now she turned in after him but went to the other side of the parking lot. She parked and squinted through the window. *Maybe he's stopping off to get some things for work — that guy in the uniform is waving at him — he knows him.*

Mary was starting to feel a bit silly, yet her curiosity still tugged at her. She watched Walter walk inside.

Maybe he has a side business. She got out of the car and walked up to the man in the uniform. The tag on his shirt said Ed. "Would you mind telling me which unit that man you were just waving at is going to? You see, he's my fiancé and — and he left his tablet behind." Ed looked kindly at her (not patronizing, the way Walter and many men she interacted with sometimes regarded her). "I'm in a bit of a hurry to get back to work…"

"Oh sure, he's got unit 3123."

Mary walked up the two flights of stairs and found herself in a long corridor lined with red roll-up doors. Having never been in one of these units before, it felt kind of exciting, like a caper from one of the books she'd read. Number 3116. *Not much farther.*

She knew she had the right unit when she bent to look up under the halfway-rolled-up door. Only Walter's legs and feet were visible, and she recognized his shoes. Instinct told her that maybe she should turn around right then and there and leave him to whatever this business was.

This isn't like me: suspicious, paranoid, needy… Maybe I'll just go back to the car…

But she'd come this far. And Mary didn't like to leave things unfinished. She crouched down to get a fuller view. Walter had his back to the door. He wasn't moving, but his arms were up, elbows sticking out on either side. It looked like both hands were on his face.

Is he crying?

Surrounding him on all three sides were racks of clothing. Women's clothing. Some of them still bore tags.

Is he running a clothing business? Why wouldn't he tell me? Is this where he got all those lovely garments? Is he embarrassed to tell me he got them wholesale?

She saw a dress that looked the same as one he gave her last month. But blue. And on the other side, a brown sweater that looked exactly the same as the green one he gave her in the spring. Some of stuff didn't look new. But it was clean.

Walter turned. He was clutching a shortie bathrobe, satin pink with little Japanese cherry blossoms all over it, firmly over his nose.

What is he…? Is he smelling *that?* Then something familiar hit her. *Samsara!*

She stood up suddenly. Walter heard her gasp. He could just make out the familiar skirt hem that fell delicately on slender calves and the one-inch-heeled pumps. *Mary!* He dropped the bathrobe and expertly rolled the door all the way up. "Mary."

But she had already bolted, careening through the hall, already at the end past the elevators, and crashing through the exit door.

'Tit Mo's Trove of
Tossed-Aside Treasures

Unit #3223: 6'×12'×8'
This medium-sized unit lovingly holds the contents of a bachelor pad or a one-bedroom.

If 'tit Mo Bouchard had his way, the first thing you'd see when sliding up the door of his family's storage unit would be his prized collection of LPs ("Not albums!"). His father, Maurice, for whom he was named (then later awarded the term of endearment "Petit Mo" — which over time got shortened even further) had kept the unit for years, even after moving to the opposite side of the city. It was a thirty-minute drive on a good day, and that was if you took the highway along the lake. They meant it to be temporary, to hold on to the types of items that normally went into an attic or garage, but their modest new bungalow had neither, and four kids with all their things filled up every inch of space.

'Tit Mo's vinyl collection ended up in the storage locker after a flood damaged his basement bedroom, mercifully leaving the milk crates full of records untouched. He had no other space for them and didn't want to sell them — he knew they were worth a lot but just couldn't bring himself to part with Zeppelin, Floyd, the Stones, the Beatles, the Doors, Lynyrd Skynyrd … all in mint condition — so they went into temporary storage. As with his family's castoffs at EZ Storage, "temporary" eventually became more than two years.

After he'd gotten one of the block's first CD players back in the eighties and seen music evolve from analogue to digital, 'tit Mo had put his no-longer-played LPs into clear plastic covers and filed them in the milk crates he began to amass. (He'd gotten his crates long before milk producers changed the size so that people would stop swiping them from outside convenience stores to use for their records.)

If 'tit Mo had his way, the next thing you'd see in the unit after his albums would be his collection of super-rare hockey cards (the Dave Keon rookie one still his most prized), which were preserved much like his LPs, each in its own clear plastic pocket within one of the black-covered albums, which also had their own dedicated crates.

Leaning up against two stacked crates was a third collection, this time of framed hockey-player posters, some even autographed, and then his framed album cover art, including the obligatory *Dark Side of the Moon* artwork and what his dad called "dat wan wit da blimp" — the replica of Led Zeppelin's debut. These had joined his records when 'tit Mo's parents informed him that they were going to start using his extra closet to house his father's beer-brewing equipment.

Once CDs morphed into MP3s, suddenly his CD collection seemed to take up too much room in his parents' basement. He'd gotten rid of all the hard plastic cases and filed the discs in those unrippable CD envelopes, arranging the liner notes in a shoebox so they were easy to find. Anything to keep space for his LPs. But with the flood, it seemed that even nature was conspiring to squeeze out his most prized possessions.

So by the time he'd traded in his iPod for a smartphone, the CDs had joined their LP compatriots in the storage locker, and 'tit Mo once again began thinking he'd likely sell them sometime — he'd just have to reunite them with their liner notes and bundle them by artist, something he had even less heart for than inventorying his LPs, given he'd likely make much less on them.

***

These days when you opened up the locker, the first things you saw would be 'tit Mo's older brother Simon's neatly stacked boxes and plastic bins, perfectly arranged by weight and size so that the heaviest, largest ones were at the bottom, supporting the smaller, lighter ones. A week after announcing that his employer was relocating him to Vancouver, Simon had hastily stacked all evidence of his life at the family home just inside the door of the unit, not bothering to move them farther in. He hadn't even put his stuff against a wall. He told his parents that it was only for a bit. "You know, until I see how much stuff I have room for in the new space."

"Vancouver's even more expensive dan Toronto!" their mother, Berthe, had exclaimed, concern threaded through her thick Québécois accent, "I've 'eard dat even places of a tousand square feet near da water, dey're going for more dan a million!"

She had read that statistic on the news ticker that continually ran like moving wallpaper in the kitchen, where Berthe could most often be found. She said she kept the news channel running 24-7 because that way she could be sure that none of the shootings, auto accidents or explosions were happening to any of *her* kids, a group which later would include her grandkids.

So Simon's boxes had been there for just over a year now. At some point, one of his parents had gone and moved them to one side — though still in the very front — just so that there was room to walk in without tripping over them. Simon's left-behinds had become somewhat of a running joke among the whole family. Even his uptight, pickle-up-her-ass sister Amélie had gotten in on the fun. "I came across a bill from the place," Mo overheard her telling Nick, her husband, as they got ready to leave after one of their typically short visits to the family homestead. "What a waste of money! They should have closed that thing down years ago." But later that week, he'd heard his father on the phone, telling her that Simon had taken over paying for the rental six months before.

Simon's boxes were now stacked higher than 'tit Mo himself who, having only gotten up to five feet, lived up (or down) both to the meaning of his term of endearment and to its having been truncated over the years — though, in his skates, he always seemed even taller than the 1.25 inches the blades would add. But he had never outgrown the rosacea that'd plagued him since middle school. This had been the subject of several ostracizations by each grade's herd of bullies, whose members may have changed from one year to the next, but whose approach toward humiliating 'tit Mo — both for his stature and for his perma-flushed cheeks — endured.

And then, of course, there was the suggestive *spelling* of his nickname, which invariably some teacher would put up on the board instead of *Maurice*; most places he went, no one knew him by his proper name. There'd always be a few kids who'd spread the word around the rest of the school each September. He should have known better than to think that little detail would be forgotten over the summer.

For the rest of the day after 'tit Mo had overheard his father on the phone telling his sister that Simon was now paying for the unit, he could feel his father's eyes burning into him whenever they were in the same room, as if to remind him that his big brother was now paying to store *his* stuff as well. Though he thought even his father could appreciate that his collection had gone up in value since the last time he'd visited the unit. That had been when he'd found — as if dropped from the sky — the Yvan Cournoyer card! It was one of those rare moments when 'tit Mo contemplated that there might just actually be a god, that his devout Catholic *maman* might just be right.

***

His parents had asked whether Simon would be coming home for Christmas that year and, muttering something about being new and having to put in extra shifts to cover his colleagues with seniority, their eldest informed them he wouldn't be able to. But he *would* use the money he saved on plane fare to pay for the next year's rental of the locker. And it was then that 'tit Mo's parents decided to start moving more items of theirs into it as well.

And so it was that 'tit Mo's treasures were shoved even farther back into the locker to make room for ancient dolls, trophies from his sisters' gymnastics competitions, Simon's old high school desk and bookshelves... All the Bouchard children were evidenced in this lot out front — all but 'tit Mo (though it made sense, given he was the only one who remained chez Bouchard so he kept most of his stuff in his basement room).

And much like his stuff in storage, 'tit Mo had always felt like an afterthought. What with Simon the Golden Boy sucking up all the air in the room, and then his sisters being twins and all.

Garcon doré… does that even work in French? he wondered.

He had never completely learned the language, being born in Toronto after his dad had been transferred to the Goodyear plant from Lachute, Québec. His parents held on stubbornly to their French when speaking to each other at home, but to help their progeny adjust to mostly Anglo Toronto, they would switch to English in front of the kids. So 'tit Mo never really got that immersion that would have made those words come more naturally.

Except of course for *les jurons* — those he knew encyclopaedically and could pronounce best, so often did he hear his dad launch into a whole string of them — and not just the terms Anglos often joked about, like *hostie* and *tabarnak*, but also other religion-based epithets: *câlice, bout d'viarge, simonac…* It happened most often on Saturday nights, whenever his beloved Habs let in a goal.

'Tit Mo grinned inwardly every time he heard that last one — *simonac* — containing as it did his brother's name. The coincidence made up slightly for the ribbing 'tit Mo endured about *his* handle.

But his siblings all held on to some of their French, enough to score way better marks than he did in the subject at school. And not speaking as much French as they did was just another knock against 'tit Mo in his mind. Golden Simon, who could do no fuckin' wrong — even though he had the personality of a pencil and almost never spoke (in any language) was always considered without fault, even while 'tit Mo brought his animated self to the dinner table each night. (Unsurprisingly, he had anxiety most of the time, which made him more talkative.)

And 'tit Mo — whom his mother sometimes called Maurice *le jeune*, in contrast to his father, Maurice *le vieux* — would also never live up to his dad's formidable presence in the Bouchard home or in the wider community. Because he was small and slight and perennially flushed, he had a youthfulness that belied his thirty-two years. And he was not brainy like his elder brother, so he wasn't going to ever get a job doing "that programming shit," as he called it. (Admittedly, neither Berthe nor Maurice le vieux knew exactly what their eldest Simon did for a living. All they knew was that it involved computers and paid well enough for him to move out to Vancouver with no second income from a wife.)

What 'tit Mo did have over his parents was that neither Bouchard son would likely ever have children — that would be their sisters' job; and indeed, Aline et Amélie (usually referred to as "*les jumelles*," even by 'tit Mo) had four between them, and there was already a great grandchild from Aline's daughter Ashlee, Aline becoming a *grand-mère* at only thirty-seven. (However ill-conceived, a true Catholic Québécois family would never begrudge someone for adding greater numbers to their brood.) He was pretty sure that his brother had ruled out the possibility of children a long time ago. He'd never caught wind of Simon dating anyone. And he'd more than once heard one of his sisters refer to Simon as a "closeted homosexual," always when their parents were far out of earshot.

The other way in which 'tit Mo knew he outdid everyone in his family — even the now-distant Simon — was in his ability to skate. He practically floated once those blades hit his feet; his usual twitchy, somewhat unnerving presence transformed into something almost otherworldly. He knew how good he was because of the way people at the rink would stop and press their noses up against the plexiglass, eyes trained on him as he warmed up before practice. Every season when a crop of peewees would arrive for their first practice, he noted a bunch of new faces lined up along the bottom row of the bleachers — both kids and parents, transfixed. The few times either of his own parents had come to the rink, even they seemed impressed at 'tit Mo's grace on the ice.

He knew that the rink manager and the City valued his being employed there as a rink guard whose role over the years had evolved into his giving private skating lessons and, not long after, becoming coach of the younger kids' teams. And in turn, they got his loyalty to the rink. A few times over the years, coaches from other rinks had shown up and tried to get him to defect. But his anxiety would bubble up until it nearly strangled him at night at the thought of having to take the transit and get up earlier for ice time. McCormick's arena was his second home. His house was just three blocks away. His life made sense. In a way that it didn't the moment he contemplated working somewhere else.

It was true that his parents had mounted some of the group photos of 'tit Mo and his skating or hockey teams alongside Simon's several degrees on the front-room mantle, next to a few of Amélie's award-winning newspaper columns and the photos of her and Aline's kids (who formed one big group of siblings in his mind).

His talent on the ice and prominence at the arena had also been why his parents had let him hang on to every pair of skates he'd outgrown, another beloved collection. But once his sisters had started to have kids, was he able to keep his army of beaten-up but beloved skates, some of which he'd had long before they'd moved to McCormick's? *Non!* "What if wan of da grandchildren or great-grandchildren came over and 'urt demselves?"

Berthe was adamant. If he wanted to keep them, they would have to join his sports and music memorabilia and collections at EZ Storage. So 'tit Mo had hung up his three most recently worn-out pairs of skates on his bedroom wall — he had to replace them every year, even though the size no longer changed. The other dozen or so pairs occupied three clear plastic containers — he'd gotten see-through ones so he'd know which ones were in each bin. They were tucked behind the place of honour held by his LPs and sports collectibles, but all this was still stuck behind Simon's boxes and his parents' more recent arrivals, which had themselves been moved deeper into the locker, behind Simon's belongings.

It was on his way to add another pair of worn-out blades, flushing as he thought about his skills as a skater and the respect he'd garnered from the local parents and kids, that 'tit Mo discovered "the rearrangement." His face turning a rare white, he kicked one of the bins. *Why are Simon's things in front and mine sent to the penalty box?*

His mother, of course. While 'tit Mo knew that his parents loved him, he also knew that Simon would always be the favourite. Indeed, in contrast with the comic potential of 'tit Mo's name, his brother's ended more definitively with *mon* — "mine."

So it was no surprise that, in an effort to somehow karmically will her eldest to come home and visit — which he had yet to do even once — Berthe had gone to the locker and, by herself, managed to have their more recently arrived things switch places with Simon's, so that all his furniture and crates were up front, carefully placed as if ready to be moved out anytime whereas 'tit Mo's skate crates had been relegated to the back with the rest of his stuff. It was as if by making Simon's stuff so easily accessible, his mother would magically compel him to return.

'Tit Mo tried hard not to be offended by these furtive acts of wishful thinking on his mom's part. He tried to convince himself that it was just another example of how stubborn she was. She'd always been the kind of person who, once she put her mind to something, could not easily be deterred. Yet Berthe's efforts with the locker assumed their place among the string of minor slights to his self-worth that had lasted as long as Maurice le jeune could remember.

But this one stung more than most. Because he was almost certain that his brother, now having shed his oppressive Catholic home, would not be returning to claim his possessions anytime soon, if ever.

And yet, along with his containers, it was like Simon was still there and always would be, overshadowing everything his little brother did.

The Siege on Steve's Stuff

Unit #3261: 10'×11'×8'
This compact unit holds two to three rooms of furniture. Up on a higher floor and with climate control, both essentials and collectibles will have a safe and dry second home.

Down the hall and to the right of one unfortunate son's storage unit was the unit of an older but also unfortunate son. Steve was middle-aged though still youthful with his slim, wiry build and full head of hair. He stood on one side of his unit and gently leaned guitar number five of eight against the others that all sat, dignified, near the front of the storage locker. He'd managed to keep the three best ones with him while he waited to save enough for a bigger place to live.

He still couldn't fucking believe the condo management had taken all his stuff and held it hostage, when he'd *told* them he'd have the money soon. He just *knew* he was going to get that tech support job. Why the fuck wouldn't they just trust him when he said he'd have the rent money soon? He just needed a bit more time.

It was his fucking cunt of an ex-wife that had reduced him to this. That stone-cold bitch had up and left him, thrown him away like it was garbage day. And then the fucking condo company locking him out of his home, stuffed his prized possessions into a couple lockers in the freezing basement. His guitars. The TV. His clothes. Video recordings of their daughter — even her first steps! — captured with the then high-end camera, circa 2009. He'd planned to transfer those recordings onto his laptop, and *maybe* give copies to Laurel. All of it in that cold basement. And to get everything back, he'd had to pay three times what this storage locker now cost for the month. They'd been real pricks with him too; it was bad enough they'd made him fuckin' homeless. They could have at least had the decency to let him move his things out first. He could have borrowed the money to get a truck if they'd given him a bit more time. At least given him some dignity, after what he'd been through; better yet, trusted him when he said he'd have the rent for them any day now. He was only behind by four months, and they'd used his last month's rent for one of them. *Wasn't the law supposed to always favour the tenant?*

But no, they'd evicted him and dumped everything he owned into a couple lockers in the basement. At least that bitch had left him with *some* of the good things. She hadn't argued when he said he'd be taking the home theatre, the basement furniture, the massive wall hanging that had been his mom's — and which he knew his ex-wife loved.

Oh, and the bed.

"Oh that. You can fuckin' have *that*. Why would I want to sleep there, now? Even if it *is* the bed we made our children in. All I feel now is disgust when I look at it."

But of course the lying bitch had been more than happy to sleep in it up to the day she took the kids and left.

Steve thought about those last few weeks in the house together — him on the pull-out in the basement, where at least there'd been the home theatre set-up (and all the porn he could consume!). Her up in the room, still up in the night sometimes with Adam, whose room was across from theirs, even though he'd stopped breastfeeding more than a year ago after turning three. And nine-year-old Sarah, who still woke sometimes.

Better she deal with it than me, he'd thought at the time. *She might as well get used to doing all the work. And boy, is she going to have trouble once it's just her and the kids — she thinks she can do all I do around here, on top of her job and the pathetic amount of housework she does now? She's so mentally unstable, she'll never be able to keep up with everything. Then it'll be my time to step in and rescue my kids.*

She'd had a truck pull up, and men who loaded their things onto it. The dining room set, most of the dishes, pots and pans, everything from the kids' bedrooms and most of what had been in theirs (other than the aforementioned bed), the china cabinet that had been his mother's. (Sentimentality aside, what TF need did he have for something like that?)

And anyway, all the valuable glass objects that had been on display on the cabinet's shelves had been lost some years earlier when one of the ancient plastic shelf brackets buckled, sending all their most fragile and valuable wedding gifts sliding down the glass, forcing the cabinet door open and smashing spectacularly onto the hardwood.

Their daughter had been less than a year old, napping in her play yard a mere foot away from where everything had landed — thank God nothing landed on her! — and had been startled into a fit of terrified screaming that had taken them forty-five minutes to quell.

The day that happened, he should have known that their marriage was doomed.

But he still had some valuable things. Like his Gibson SG. Hell, he'd had that before the name *Laurel* had taken up residence in his mind. He'd gotten to keep that (*thank fuck!*) even when he was at his financial worst. No way he was going to hawk that guitar unless he was starving on the street. He thought it would end up a write-off, what with the freezing conditions in the basement — the wood on that baby was surely going to buckle. But it had survived. He'd also been able to keep his convertible. They couldn't touch that.

Oddly, the enduring nature of his guitar reminded him of little Sarah and Adam's fish. It hadn't moved out when the children had. Little Sarah and her mother came back for Fishie a week later. That half-inch-long zebra-striped swimmer had survived a lot. It had been one of about twenty shiny multi-hued tropical fish — all of which had eventually been eaten or succumbed after eating others — who knew why. The plecostomus, the one who was supposed to keep the tank clean, he'd been the first to go, having gorged on the algae that lined the inside walls. They figured the surplus algae had come from the little ten-gallon tank being right in the path of the afternoon sunbeams. And he was supposed to be the one that would hoover up the buildup to clean the tank! (Did he maybe overeat? Maybe sucked onto the gravel and swallowed some fish shit?) And yet through the loss of his kin and the maintenance crew, even smaller than most of the others, somehow Fishie had triumphed. And now he had the entire ten gallons to himself.

I'm like that fish, thought Steve the day they came to get it. *I may not be going with them to the new house, but I'll survive anything they throw at me now.*

It'd been too unwieldy to move the fish the same day as everything else, so he'd said that Daddy would take care of Fishie until they could come back and get it. And that gave him another chance to see his little girl back in their house. Laurel had been smart (or hateful enough, he couldn't decide) not to come out of the car, so he'd had to bring the tank out, Sarah trailing behind with the pump, heater, gravel and fake plants.

For those twenty minutes with Sarah in what was still their house, he could imagine that nothing had changed, even with most of the furniture gone and the bare nails and hooks that had held so many school photos and vacation pictures (except that wall hanging of his mom's ... he'd *never* let her have *that* one).

With his little Sarah there, he could keep imagining that Laurel hadn't changed her bank account and phone number five months earlier, even after he'd said he'd go to counselling; that he hadn't had to cower in the garage every time their agent brought new potential buyers tramping through their family home; that she wasn't taking Sarah and Adam; that he was not going to have to figure out where to live so he could have them over.

But he *had* landed okay, a month later. The condo had been the ideal choice: a five-minute drive from the house Laurel rented, with underground parking for his Bimmer (she'd let him walk away with one reward out of the piddly proceeds of their house sale); and it was newly built, way nicer than the rundown house Laurel had rented. Before moving out, she'd also traded in their Tercel and gone and bought herself a brand-new 4Runner, then told him — to his great surprise — that he was not ever going to drive it. Ever!

So he'd needed — no, *deserved* — a treat, after all she'd put him through. It didn't matter that he hadn't found work; the bank believed him when he said he was good for the loan. Because even with what that woman had reduced him to, he knew he could come back from anything. It wasn't *his* fault she'd made things so difficult for him for *years* before this that he'd not managed to focus enough to get or keep a job. Plus her business was doing well, so why should he have to settle for just any job? Better to hold out for something more suited to his exceptional talent.

He felt like *Steve* again, the guy he'd been before Laurel; before kids. Not *Stephen*. Not the name his aggravating mother would insist everyone call him each time she met a new one of his friends. His mother had a storage unit at EZ as well, something Steve took great pains to put out of his mind. He viewed this fact as the only similarity between them. After all, *he* had his stuff here because of his ex-wife — and would be using it again, damn soon! And with the discount from the Hurwitzes, it made sense to store his stuff a bit out of the way of his place in North Toronto. Plus he knew all the jobs with the six-figure salaries were near the financial district, which was only twenty or so minutes away from Coxwell and Lakeshore.

Marla, well she was an entirely different story; for her, it was stuff from *more than twenty-five fucking years ago*, when his parents divorced! Her child-support payment from his dad had dried up when his sister moved out with her fiancé, and Mom had moved back in with her own mother, eventually moving most of her things from the apartment to EZ Storage. All those things that she'd kept for years, cluttering her succession of two-bedrooms in a way that offended Steve. He'd vowed never to end up like that. But then, didn't he and Laurel end up fighting about as much as *his* parents had?

So Mom had kept that unit for more than twelve fuckin' years now. And every few months he would hear — from different relatives in their turn — about how she'd missed a bunch of bills in a row for what became known as "the locker." And could he chip in and pay for it this time? His sister Helen had already paid the bill for the past six months; before that, his uncle John had saved many a day. The subject of the locker had morphed into the family's figurative hot potato.

The woman was so stuck in the past. Bitter. And she had no need for most of the crap she had in there. The fucking dining room set from when he'd been twelve, the one that went with the unfortunate china cabinet his wife now had. (She'd had the shelf's brackets and missing panes of glass repaired, so she'd said it was more hers by the time they left than it was his.)

His younger sister, much as she had liked some of his mom's paintings, wanted nothing to do with "her old shit." *God knows Mom doesn't even go in to clean up or to take anything out*, he thought. *She just adds more crap.* Last time it'd been a collection of CD jewel cases — two file boxes full — because she'd put all the CDs in a soft case but still wanted to have the original cover art and lyric sheets.

"At least *some* CDs still have the artwork and information that albums used to!" she'd say in that nasal whine, with that indignant tone.

His sisters had finally cleaned out that locker last month. They'd managed to find some of his hockey card collections that his mother had missed when she'd last visited. *They'd been salvaged!* But of course, his mother had stuffed a few of the albums inside flimsy file boxes, and now several cards were unaccounted for.

He'd discovered this unfortunate fact when he opened the album at the top of the pile and noticed the first page was missing a couple of cards — and he knew his collection had been immaculate — and being near the front, they were among his most valuable. One of the losses was the 1964 Yvan Cournoyer his grandfather had given to his mom to hold on to for him, long before Steve could even remember watching his first NHL game. The year "The Roadrunner" made MVP! How careless could she be? Hadn't he already lost enough?

He'd only been to the locker a handful of times: once to move all his stuff in and a few other times to grab some things for his new place, the furnished basement that was only a stepping stone for now. Most of the stuff in the unit wouldn't fit into his place, and furniture was provided, including a futon and a pullout couch left behind from the previous tenant, so he'd come back for a few important things: his two best guitars; an amp and some cords; his interview suits and some casual stuff, along with some of his kids' clothes (he hoped they'd still fit!); blanket, pillow; a few of his son's puzzles; some Lego; a baseball bat and ball.

He really looked forward to Sarah and Adam's visits. Being evicted put a real wrench into his regular time with his littles. Laurel had at least been reasonable about letting him see them every week. But he didn't like the way she'd text him almost every time, asking him to confirm whether and what time he was coming to get the kids.

Why do I have to confirm with her? I shouldn't have to make an appointment to see my own children!

And they idolized him, he could feel it. Even when he'd lost his place and had to go stay with Helen for a few months before moving here, they couldn't wait to see him, and they jumped all over him every time he pulled up to get them. They loved being in his car with the top down; he was really dreading the arrival of winter.

I bet they aren't nearly as happy with that mother of theirs, now they see what she's really like.

And he always felt so proud to drive by people, his beautiful children's hair being blown back. When he'd pull up to a stoplight, sometimes there'd be a woman in the car next to him who'd look over with that face women get when they see puppies. It was great for his prospects.

The few times he'd been to EZ Storage, he'd passed that security guard. Al, was it? No, Ed. Whatever. The guy seemed pretty cool, even if he looked a bit awkward at times for reasons Steve could only guess at. Maybe Ed was intimidated by him. Steve was clearly much more intelligent than a mere security guard. Or maybe he was still holding a grudge against him. The last time Steve had been there, he thought Ed was giving him a dirty look. It made him wonder if maybe this guy should be trusted to guard his stuff and all those other people's — the place said it had 425 units. At least there were cameras trained on some of the main spots: the elevators, exit doors from each floor, the main entrance, the back loading bay and those elevators too. And if the facility was big, so was Ed. Probably had more brains in his biceps. Anyway, Steve had no reason to really talk with the guy.

But there had been that one time he'd gone to the locker, when he'd first met Ed. That visit was before his stuff had been moved in. It was about his mother. His sister and uncle had made their regular call to him, this time saying they'd gotten together on it and were trying to get Marla to start donating or selling her things. They'd finally taken the hard line Steve had been telling them to take for a couple years now.

They made it clear that either she should get in there and take what she still needed, and they'd get a truck to come get the rest, or they'd just let the management company for the unit get rid of everything. Steve was happy to see that for once his family had seen how right he was. *As is usually the case — if only they saw it!*

And as always happened, he and his mother had gotten into a screaming match in front of the office after she'd met him there but said she'd *changed her mind*; she couldn't go up to the locker that day; it was just too painful. He'd told her she really had no choice, and if she didn't take this chance to go see what she wanted to keep, that'd be it.

How stupid could she be?

So it was that day that he'd met Ed, who didn't seem like he worked there yet. Ed may have had about fifty pounds on him, but Steve was pretty sure he could take him. But it just wasn't worth it, especially when Ike Hurwitz joined the fray — so he just decided to head back to his car and tear away, making sure to squeal his tires.

He was pretty sure it was the next time he went there that Ed had given him the look. If only the guard knew what a psycho Steve's mother was, maybe he wouldn't be so quick to judge. At this point Steve was convinced he'd spent his entire life *surrounded* by psychotic women! The one thing he *did* know: He wouldn't end up like his hoarder mother. He was going to get all *his* things back once he'd been at his job long enough to get a bigger place. And then his kids wouldn't have to sleep on the pullout anymore. They'd have their own room. And they'd see that *he* was the one they wanted to live with.

Things had gotten more complicated lately, with Laurel serving him papers about custody and child support. The bitch hired a lawyer. They had a court date in three weeks. Three weeks! Like he was going to have time to prepare his defence; like he had any money right now to hire a lawyer. He'd already tapped his uncle and sisters and his best friend, Mark. But he needed that money to live.

And she'd fuckin' told him in one of their many rapid-fire fights over text that she had no doubt she'd get custody. Not only because he had *broken them financially*, but because he'd been *verbally and physically abusive*. Hah! All he'd done was throw a few things at her when she'd pushed him to his limit. Oh, and that time she'd broken her finger when he'd closed a door on her to keep her from screaming at him yet again. It was her own fault. She was a crazy bitch! And who puts their hand on a door jamb when someone is slamming against the door? Fucking typical of her, trying to nail him when he was at his worst. He didn't have time to go to court or that mandatory information night.

If I don't show up, what's the worst that can happen? There's no way they'll just give the kids to her. But then the courts usually do favour the mother — but not one as unhinged as Laurel.

And surely they'd see that he'd been scraping the ground financially since his family had left him, that he wouldn't be obligated to pay child support until he'd gotten time to repair this life that his wife had rampaged.

Whatever happened, he'd fix it come that day when his shit was back together. And then he'd take that cunt back to court and *prove* he was the more stable one, that she was a loose cannon — hadn't she proven that by how she'd snatched his children away from him?

He just needed a bit more time.

***

Four months later, affronted and discouraged, Steve dropped by EZ Storage to get out another guitar he'd been missing. It made him feel like shit, being there again and not yet ready to move the rest of the unit's contents into the two-bedroom he'd been looking for.

On the way up he shared an elevator with a younger-looking man who got off on the second floor, not looking up, pushing a dolly stacked with four grey Rubbermaid bins.

What a loser, thought Steve, suddenly not feeling as sorry for himself. Can't even look a man in the eye.

Allowances for Anxious Audrey

Unit #2201: 6'×12'×8'
This mid-sized unit holds what you would fit into a room the size of a typical den or man cave.

Full to the top, Toby's storage locker contained perfectly stacked boxes and plastic bins he'd bought to nest together, all grey with clear lids. If anyone had one of those X-ray machines, like they used in the airport security gates, they'd see that everything inside had been meticulously arranged to fill out all the space it could within the boxes and bins: books, used notebooks, writing materials, videotapes and DVDs (in alpha order, *natch*, with the discs removed from their cases, put into liners and stored in groups of a hundred and carefully arranged in shoeboxes).

They'd also see the lovingly wrapped characters from *Star Wars*, *Superman* and *Star Trek*, no longer holding their place of pride on the shelves of their owner's man cave. And then there was the alphabetically sorted array of Every Movie Stanley Kubrick Made (including director's cuts and special editions complete with commentary). With streaming now yielding any film he could search up, Toby really only needed these for display purposes. Much as he treasured his collections — knowing they'd be worth a lot of money someday (assuming he could ever bring himself to fully part with them), Toby knew they were not as important to him as his most valued treasure: his sweet, brilliant Audrey.

***

Audrey had anxiety. Crippling anxiety. When Toby would mention that she might need a support group (which he did every few months or so, in a rare display of self-determination), she would recoil as if in horror of anything that smacked of AA. Because that sounded too much like "Anxious Audrey," the nickname her brother, Alastair, had given her from as far back as she could remember. While only eleven months apart, the two could not have been more different from one another.

Indeed, Al, who'd settled for the most ordinary of names and lifestyles, seemed content to go home every night, twist up a spliff, crack open a cold one, and watch reality shows and *Home Improvement* reruns with his girlfriend. It reminded Audrey of a Facebook meme, something about the unintelligent living much happier lives because they were blithely oblivious to how much they didn't know.

At thirty-six, Audrey had still not completely managed to conquer her anxiety — that menacing, buzzy-headed brain fog alternating with stomach-seizing waves of panic that hovered over her almost every day for as long as she could remember, clenching her gut even harder anytime she started thinking about how she would approach her next task or situation.

Even after taking a home-based editing job a couple pay grades beneath her experience just so she could work nearly in private, she regularly endured an unrelenting sense of foreboding anytime she had to speak in virtual meeting rooms. Even after she and Toby made the decision not to have children, since she worried both about her ability to raise a child and whether their child might inherit the same fear she walked around with. Even after she'd had stretches of time where her thoughts and actions seemed to arrive spontaneously, without the usual ruminations, giving her weeks of relief and hope for going on to something more fulfilling in her life.

Even with all the accommodations she'd made with Toby's support and with those merciful periods of relief, she'd still get seized by that all-too-familiar anxiety. Again and again.

***

The White Room had been Toby's idea — after she'd descended into one of the worst funks he'd seen in the four years he'd been with Audrey. He liked that it gave her a safe space, and it bore the name of a really cool Cream song.

He'd made the decision to empty out his former den when he'd gotten home one Friday afternoon. Alternately pacing and walking in circles — "wearing a hole in the rug," as his mother would have said — was how Toby found Audrey as, six pack in hand, he soundlessly closed the apartment door. (Audrey didn't like being startled, so he'd had a special noise-free latch installed shortly after she'd moved in.)

At this point they'd only been living together a few months. She'd been afraid of that too.

It was a one-bedroom and den, which he'd had for seven years and which had always been both clean *and* tidy. Even the den, Toby's man cave, belied its name, so neatly assembled and alphabetized were his vintage *Star Wars* figures and *Star Trek* bobbleheads. He'd liked the location too, only a few blocks east of Pape Station, a new development at the time he'd moved in.

But then Audrey came and needed a home office, so she set up in the den. Though there was room in their living area, she'd said she needed a place with a door that closed. So he'd let her place her desk and filing cabinet among his media centre — the home theatre and stereo, speakers on custom shelving, video box sets placed lovingly on a side bookshelf, mainly for display purposes — then watched for months as her piles began to spawn like troublesome tribbles, overtaking the former glory of his lovingly placed objects and forcing him to move his La-Z-Boy out into the living room.

Her piles of paper and file boxes — they had no logic to them! And didn't she do most of her work online? It hadn't seemed as bad when she'd lived at her own place; but then she'd kept her office door closed and they'd spent most of their time in the living room and bedroom. Her home had always felt smaller and more cramped than his, but he'd figured it was because it was in an older house with smaller rooms.

So when he came up with the White Room idea, it was just as much for him as for her, so tired was he of watching the series of unevenly stacked leaning towers grow with each passing month. Toby would find himself almost toppling them as he passed.

And maybe, Toby had thought, *if I give her a space that's nice and uncluttered, with my wall shelves empty and the white vintage IKEA bookshelf — maybe she'll feel less cluttered in her mind too.* And once that happened, she'd start to arrange her office and, feeling calmer and at home, would finally start to relax and be more like the version of Audrey he'd fallen for. And maybe someday soon he'd ask her to make it official.

The White Room was Toby's act of love, his protective shroud. He'd given the walls a fresh coat of Whitest White and gotten a billowy set of sheer drapes hung, just for her, again hoping to give the room an air of calm and openness that she couldn't have experienced among the more masculine energy of his grey roller blinds, home theatre objects, and science fiction action figure collections.

And though it pained him not to have these items where he could admire them, he decided to get a storage locker for them, for the time being. There, they could be wrapped up and properly put away, protected from potential dampness and floods — not crammed together to fit into their condo's damp locker room. He'd chosen the slightly more costly second-floor unit because it was climate controlled and there was no chance of flooding. (The guy at EZ Storage had warned him that ground-floor units were better for things that would normally go into a garage.)

If they got married, he'd bring his treasured collection back, set it up in the house they'd get. Or maybe sell them for some money to put toward the down payment ... if he could bear to part with them by then.

He'd always known about Audrey's tendency to be nervous, but figured that — what with his OCD tendencies — who was *he* to judge? It took one broken person to truly understand and help another one, right? And since he hadn't had anxiety attacks for years, surely he could help her get over hers. And it would start with him giving her some space that was all her own.

But he didn't expect the piles would start to build, as if made mightier as they filled all the clear floor space and storage shelves he'd put in. *How does an editor, who cleans up other people's writing and follows rigid editing rules, end up being so sloppy with her own stuff?* She hadn't even bothered to try and arrange anything on the wall shelves. The closet organizer he'd added? Empty.

It seemed to get even worse after her father passed, not long after she'd moved in. Dick hadn't had much, so there was nothing expected to come to Audrey from him (even though she was an only child). The burial arrangements had been taken care of by Audrey's uncle Len, who — while he didn't keep in touch with Dick's ex-wife or daughter — had always been in touch by cheque, anytime their family had been in a jam, which was often.

Audrey's mother had long since remarried and could mostly be reached on Instagram these days, where a carousel of photos showed her standing in the background of her husband's effusive posts about this or that world monument they'd "conquered" on that month's bucket list.

By the time they'd agreed to cohabit, Audrey had already been used to being alone a lot in her cramped rental. Even though he knew about her anxiety, Toby still thought her to be one of the bravest and most self-sufficient people he knew — *he* hadn't moved out on his own until he was twenty-five, leaving behind a nuclear family of two parents and two younger siblings.

So he was knocked off balance when Audrey's descent into her protective pit started, about a month after Dick's funeral.

As the piles grew, so did Audrey's level of distraction. Mostly, she was monosyllabic for much of the evenings, which he at first attributed to fatigue. And maybe she was having some trouble adjusting to sharing space with him. She'd always been more of an introvert, so he expected to find her home at the end of the day. But now, a few weeks after he'd set up the White Room, she'd stopped making dinner, watching TV or even listening to the radio, like she'd usually be doing after clocking out. It being winter, he would arrive at six to a darkened apartment, finding her more often than not laid out on their living room couch, arms frozen at either side, face up toward the ceiling. She was always awake, as he'd learn when her voice weakly broke into the void: "Did you have a nice day?"

He could tell she only half-listened to his answer. She wouldn't even turn her head while he shed his boots and coat before heading to the kitchen drawer to find a take-out menu. (He still preferred to go get his food. Why pay a premium for Uber Eats or DoorDash when he could be there and back in fifteen minutes? Plus then he could check the bag to make sure they hadn't forgotten anything.)

On weekends, after they'd slept in and gone out to their regular local brunch haunt, she would bury herself in the latest book she was reading, barely speaking or leaving the couch as he came and went. Or she'd have a nap. They'd do basic house chores and shop together, but that was the only time she seemed interested in spending time with him, other than when she'd emerge for dinner and then, sometimes, later silently cuddle up next to him for a movie.

And their sex life — never a huge driver of their relationship — but the sex had always been amazing (and was one of the few times Audrey dropped her guard). Well that seemed like it had gotten packed away and sent off to EZ Storage too. He assumed this was just Audrey's way of dealing with unresolved grief over her father's passing.

It was on a Saturday morning that he started to understand, when she finally broke down into unintelligible sobs after he asked if she wanted to try a new breakfast place. This was more than her usual garden-variety anxiety at play.

"I-I just can't explain why this is happening. I'm not unhappy living with you. Actually, the opposite!" she reassured him. "But I can't make any decisions. About anything. I just feel paralyzed most of the time. Every time I look at something or listen to the news, the TV ... just, *anything* ... this scary feeling takes over, like I wonder, *How did the designer of that book figure out how to do that and how did they have the confidence to follow through? I wouldn't be able to do that if I tried to.*"

Toby, thinking it wasn't yet his turn to speak, blinked at her and nodded encouragingly.

"Then on the news or the radio, they'll be talking about someone — you know, the latest tweet or video that's gone viral — and I can't stop wondering how *they* got on the radio, how *they* managed to make the decision to do that. And if they're on the radio, and people are paying attention to them, they must be happy ... doing what they're good at and feeling good about it. And people paying attention to them. And their lives are better because people like them. They're making a difference." She wrung her hands and looked vaguely toward the floor. "Meantime, I can't even manage to clean my office. The office you made so nice for me. Everything I try to do to make things better around me, I just freeze up!"

She gulped in a teary breath. "How can I figure out what I'm supposed to be doing in the world to … to make a difference? 'Cause if I don't, then I'm nothing. Uncle Len always had told me, 'You're different from the rest of your family. You're going to make something of your life.' What would he think if he saw me now?"

Audrey fell into the nearest chair, then looked down at her open hands. "Here I am in my little room, surrounded by these piles of paper, not able to think of *one* interesting or original thing I want to do. And everything I *have* to do seems like the most monumental hurdle, the worst drudgery, so much 'sound and fury, signifying nothing.'" Toby didn't bother to mention that he liked how she'd inserted the Shakespeare reference; he still didn't want to interrupt her tearful confession.

"I don't know if … if it's because my dad is gone now or what," she said. "But I can't stop feeling like I'm completely alone. Everyone has activities, ideas…" Toby, agape, hadn't moved. "I just feel … empty. And everything that comes makes my mind flood with fear. If I were put on the spot, I wouldn't know the first place to start. All these people on social media, they're just threatening … phantom demanders … I can't even bring myself to look at the alerts on my phone or check the time when I wake up … I don't want to have to think about what's on my phone; the brain flood will get worse…"

"But you manage to get your work in every day, don't you?" Toby asked, when she finally seemed to have calmed down enough for him to get a word in.

"Barely. I calm down for long enough to get the mechanical parts done — because I know we have to survive, and after all these years there's a lot of my job I can do on autopilot. But anything that requires original thought … it's like even the decision about whether to wear the blue or black pants is life or death!"

Toby looked confused, with that expression he always had when Audrey would try to explain why she had retreated to the couch or was dissolving into tears in the middle of dinner. "And you're sure it's nothing *I've* done. Or that I haven't done?" He'd asked this before. She would always rush to reassure him.

"No. You know I've been like this my whole life. I get better for a few years, life seems normal, and I go about my business more or less happy. Like when I met you. You know all this." She'd started to pace, wearing yet another hole in the floor. "And you know that for whatever reason — usually when there are major changes in my life — I start to question everything again, and the panic comes flooding back. And it just keeps getting worse and worse until every action and decision brings another wave of anxiety. I know I should find a therapist again. But even that seems like more than I can handle and just reminds me what a fuck-up I am!"

***

Audrey had tried meds about a decade earlier — during a particularly bad case of panic attacks when she was in grad school — but found they gave her so many other symptoms. "Side effects," her GP had casually replied, when she'd inquired two weeks into starting treatment.

Yeah, like *she* knew what it was like to feel like ants were crawling over you and the world floated by in slow motion every time you turned your head, like it needed a couple seconds to catch up to where your gaze landed. And then those jolts, like electric shocks.

If there was anything Audrey could not stand, it was feeling like she had no control over her mind. So she'd closed the book on meds with a resounding crash and would hear no more of it from either the GP or the psychiatrist she'd later been referred to. That might work for Toby — he had OCD — but she was not going to let herself be drugged up just because certain situations made her nervous. She was going to be smart enough to figure it out on her own. So when her therapist retired a few years later, she'd declined a further referral.

After that she had made her life decisions based on keeping her anxiety at bay. That's how she'd manage it. Her uncle had even paid for her undergrad in English and then a master's in comparative lit. When asked if she wanted to stay on as a TA and continue to her PhD, she'd declined and started a job as a junior editor at a trade publication house instead.

After defending her thesis on quixotic characters in present-day novels, she'd started having panic attacks again and decided maybe it was time to get a real job. And start writing her first novel — which, a mere 179 pages in, had been shelved a couple years back, once she'd gotten promoted to senior editor. She'd just found it too hard to be creative and keep writing after already staring at a sea of words all day.

And then there'd been her fledgling relationship with Toby which, before they moved in together, had her out of the house a few nights a week. So, by the time they moved in together, she'd all but lost touch with — and interest in — her novel's characters. The few times she'd pulled up the files with the idea of maybe restarting the work, she'd been seized by such a feeling of dread threaded with panic that she'd abruptly slam the laptop shut. One time she'd knocked over her chair in her haste to flee the scene of her chronic procrastination. (Toby had later picked up the chair but, kindly, had not mentioned it afterward.)

In the days she was still trolling social media, she'd read a meme on an old high school friend's Facebook feed: *Not my circus, not my monkeys.* She liked that one. But what if it *was* your monkey? How did a person quell the trapeze artists and creepy clowns invading their brain *then*?

She remembered another saying she liked (though had never found a way to use): *This isn't my first rodeo.* Indeed, Audrey had ridden the bull of the Major Anxious-Depressive Episode about three times now through her adult life.

But the symptoms had alighted on her well before her first diagnosis. Her mind could trace the path back to the first anxiety attack she remembered having, when she was only twelve.

She'd been on vacation with her uncle Len. It had been her uncle's gift to her and her brother, but mostly for her, when she'd gotten all As in Grade 6. Since their parents had never been able to take the two siblings on a "real vacation" — being stuffed in the back of a station wagon for three hours heading north on the 400 notwithstanding — their uncle offered to take the kids to his regular mid-winter haunt in Cuba with him and his current arm decoration. (These much-younger women usually hung around for a couple years, then when one was gone, a new one seemed to pop out of the same mould, like a fresh angel food cake.)

Uncle Len would never really introduce any of them, making them feel even more interchangeable. It was more like "Alastair, can you pass Candace the butter?" the first time they'd sit down to a meal, or "Audrey, bring Sunny her sweater, please."

They'd gone to a resort (which there were a lot fewer of back then). And the all-inclusive variety didn't seem to register on Len's radar. He was loaded after all. Audrey gleaned this from one of her parents' many whispered discussions about Len's latest contribution to "the care and rearing of our bloodline" (Len's words) and his "trying to buy their love by spoiling them" (her father's).

They were at a restaurant — one of the expensive ones where you needed a reservation — on their last night of the trip, a Saturday. By that final dinner, everyone around the table had pretty much said all they were going to say to each other. And since they would have to get up early to fly the next day, it would be an early night. Len's latest paramour (whose name Audrey could not recall to this day. Missy? Bunny?) was inspecting her fake nails with exaggerated focus.

The trip had been fun during the first few days, but that night, they were done. And Alastair had been making noises for the last two days about missing his bed. At the table next to them was a family of six. A woman who looked to be in her early twenties and a girl a few years older than Audrey had their backs toward her. Two younger girls, probably about ten or eleven, were facing her, and a middle-aged man and woman sat at the heads of the table. Unlike Audrey's group, theirs was a flurry of activity, with several conversations going on at once.

The group had sat down around the same time they did, but she'd only noticed them once her family had finished eating and become motionless. Uncle Len had signalled the waiter for the bill, his jaw looking more clenched with each minute they sat waiting.

Meanwhile, the neighbouring table didn't look finished yet. The man was ordering more wine, telling the waiter they had just arrived yesterday and would be there until the following Saturday — as if letting them know they'd be serving him again soon. The two younger kids were being brought sundaes. (They didn't even have to share!) While Len was generous, he was still strict when it came to things not going to waste, so would make them share whatever dessert they got. And it being their final night, he'd been more low-key on the extravagance in general.

The older woman was wearing a denim dress that looked like a long man's shirt with a turquoise studded belt. Her brown shoulder-length hair was down and windswept. She was maybe fifty, maybe more, from what twelve-year-old Audrey could tell. The adolescent girl sitting closest to her was beaming in her direction. She must have been the woman's daughter.

Audrey had started to focus in on their conversation as her party continued to wait for the bill, Uncle Len's foot-tapping being the only sound from their table. At one point, all the crosstalk at the table overlapped to the point of it being impossible to make out any single conversation, so Audrey had started to gaze blankly toward the ocean as Uncle Len's foot-tapping got a bit faster. She was jolted back to the present when the woman began to laugh.

It was an awful laugh — a croaky *haaah-haaah-haaaaaah* sort of cackle. The woman looked across the table toward the man, her eyes bright. That expression, along with her messy hair and shiny cheeks, made her look like she didn't care what anyone else thought. And the two young girls were smiling in her direction as if she was their fairy godmother, the remains of their ice cream sundaes now melted into a brownish-grey pool in front of them.

Then the woman began to speak, her voice almost as grating as her laugh. "When I met your dad two years ago, he was on a shoot my job had sent me to. I really liked that job." The woman's mouth corners turned down slightly as she looked away at nothing. When she turned back to the table, she brightened again. "But my new one's pretty good too." The man raised his glass and smiled. The child closest to her then leaned over and whispered in her ear.

"Yes of course you can both sleep in the big room tonight!" the woman exclaimed, her eyes directed across the table at the man before she looked back indulgently at the pair of girls.

It occurred to Audrey at that moment that maybe this family hadn't always been together. It sounded like the trip might be the first time they had travelled together. The two younger girls appeared to be in the throes of fresh bonding. A sleepover in the big room. How lucky for them!

Whatever was fact or just assumptions borne of her adolescent imagination, there was one thing Audrey did know: This family had fun together, and they had more exciting activities and *togetherness* ahead of them. She and her brother, on the other hand, were already coming back down to earth during this last, almost wordless dinner, and would by tomorrow at this time be dumped back at home by Len's rented car, Len having hailed a separate one for himself and Bunny (or whatever her name was).

It had taken a few years of therapy before she could recall this first panic attack and recognize it as such.

At first Audrey thought she was just jealous. But it wasn't jealousy that made the blood rise into her face and the sound of her heartbeat become deafening (although jealousy likely did play into it). No. The feeling she had was shame. Shame about the place she'd come from and, by extension, about herself.

Now, decades later, she couldn't think of why she'd need to be ashamed or anxious after this many years and the trust built between her and Toby (it'd taken him a full year to convince her to give notice on her apartment). But it wasn't for no reason that the word *triggered* existed — and the changes befalling her family, combined with moving in with Toby ... it was just so much swirling in her head. And he'd gone and made it harder by clearing out his beloved collection and making up the office for her. It just felt like more pressure!

After her tearful confessions, she had begged off dinner and headed straight into their room. She lay there for hours, thinking about all that they'd talked about, all she'd revealed. And now a newer source of concrete anxiety threatened to set upon them, one that she and Toby hadn't really talked about yet, except in passing: People had been getting really sick all over the world for a few months, and now, thanks to some international travellers, this contagious illness they were calling "the coronavirus" was in Canada.

Audrey had enough trouble getting used to the idea of her dad gone, adjusting to working from what she still considered to be Toby's place. One of the many ways she'd tried to still the torrent in her head was to stop listening to the morning newscast — but news of this virus had become nonstop, even on the classical and jazz FM music stations, whose programs seemed to keep getting interrupted by more and more dire predictions.

And the past couple mornings, she'd had to spend about a half hour reading through announcements from her employer, fearful missives about *quarantining* and *stopping the spread*. Soon, one notice said, the entire staff would have to start working from home, one hundred percent of the time. How were they going to keep working that way? Could the company survive? She was used to being at home a lot, but being *forced* to stay there? Would she be out of a job on top of everything else? Might she or Toby catch the virus?

And with Toby working in IT, no doubt they'd quickly figure out what he'd need to start working from home too. Every day. Him and her. In each other's way. 24-7.

Nowhere to hide now. Or during those times when she felt straightjacketed to the couch and had to talk herself off of it. (She'd been amazed at how long it was possible to stay in one position.)

Meanwhile, as he darkened the living room in their already dead-quiet apartment and headed to their bedroom, Toby wondered, *Will I ever get my Audrey back? Will I ever stop paying for unit 2201?*

And if this virus thing he'd been hearing about was as bad as they said, and he had to start working from home … what would happen to them then? Audrey was already practically a shut-in. But quarantine? This could be the last straw that broke her (and them) for good.

Quinn's Quarantine Quandary

Unit #2210: 6'×12'×8'
This cute unit holds what you would fit into a petite bachelorette or a large closet. A good size space for someone just starting out.

Grab all seven black garbage bags and a few boxes filled with everything I own. Carry the whole pile out to the back alley to meet the Uber. (Thank the goddess it's a van!) Tie the thick scarf snugly over my nose and mouth. The driver tosses the last few bags into the back, where I offer to sit as well. He seems grateful as he heads back up to the front and starts the engine.

"Could you open the window so I can take the scarf off my face and breathe for a bit?" The driver cracks the middle side window an inch. By this time, a month into the pandemic, he's probably gotten used to people asking for open windows in winter.

This was not how I expected to move out of here. It's nothing like the many bird-flipping fantasies I've entertained each time psychopath Landlady Lydia would scowl at me in our shared laundry room or when her nasty cooking smells would come wafting up. Lockdown or not, the woman never left her basement apartment.

The shifty shut-in inherited the building when her parents died and converted the shoe-repair shop into apartments, installing her nephew above the store and reno'ing the main floor for a rental. I liked the area when I moved in a year and a half ago, and the shop window was funky and let in lots of light. It was near enough to the Beaches to get to the Queen car, but not so close that I'd pay, like, seven hundred more a month. Plus it came with furniture — some of it retro — so it was a good first apartment for me, after having only rented rooms before that.

Once Trudeau started issuing travel warnings, and later when they started using the word *pandemic*, I knew the coronavirus was an actual, like, thing. So when Lydia came to evict me literally two days after that first announcement — "I am no longer comfortable sharing my home with anyone outside my family" — I was way more willing than I shoulda been. "That virus might get into our furniture, in your unit too, and start to enter the air ducts. With my heart condition, I can't risk getting your germs." Normally I'd have reported her; only thirty fucking days' notice! But I was no more eager to be in lockdown with her underneath me than she was with me on top of her.

And until five days ago, I had a place to crash.

The plan seemed tight: My co-worker, Lee, was gonna rent me the space in her mom's basement while I figured out my next move. I'd have a bathroom, if not a kitchen. Whatever — I planned to get my food delivered. Having just been laid off herself, Lee's mom really could use the money.

Just as important, she didn't care that I'm queer. She only cared that I'd be quiet and not hang out upstairs while her own family was in quarantine. She didn't have to worry: I'm fine wearing earbuds, and Lee and I could at least meet out front or out back.

But then Lee's widowed aunt who lived about an hour away started making noises about being afraid all alone (though, according to Lee, she was probably just relishing another chance to be a massive drama queen). But Lee's mom "just couldn't say no," and there was only room in their basement for one person whose handle started with *qu*: so Quarantine Drama Queen won out over Queer but Quiet Quinn.

I'm SO sorry Quinnee! [Icy-blue horror-frown emoji].

I figured Lydia would be reasonable, knowing I had no place to go. Especially since I also lost my job after being evicted. Being a resto server, only in my current gig since last fall, I was one of the first to go. But Lydia has three older brothers who fight all her battles — including this one. "Don't even bother coming to me with that landlord-tenant act story. My brothers'll have your shit packed and outta here faster than you can start tapping out a complaint. And they're more than happy to mask up and throw you out on your bony ass along with it. And don't you even *try* to record me!"

"I wasn't—" She slammed the door in my face. And that was that.

So here I am, on the way to put my stuff into storage. No backup plan, still only half-believing this isn't some post–April fool's joke. *How the fuck did people stuck on cruise ships in Japan lead to me being both unemployed and homeless?*

Two years ago it might have been easier to deal with the situation, when my dad and stepmom still lived here. But now they live in Arizona, their newly adopted home warmer than the reception I ever got from the new wife.

"Honey, don't you have friends in your ... um, *community* ... who can help you get this sorted out?" said my dad when I called him for help. "Let me see if any of Tasha's kids can do something for you."

Ah ... Stepmommy's kids, who'd extended an even frostier welcome to the skinny dyke with the blue buzzcut and the arts degree. But they're older, settled, so they might have some room. Still, figuring that out will take time, the way that whole circus show operates.

It stung to hear his weak rationalization, but I kinda get it. No one's allowed to cross the border, and Dad doesn't have any property here, with Mom gone five years now.

I applied for the government benefit — only two thousand bucks a month, not like I make much more than that anyway — but where the hell am I going to stay until I find another home? What hotel won't charge over a hundred a night? And are hotels even offering rooms right now?

At least the bitch gave me back my last month's rent. But where am I gonna come up with first month's?

These are my thoughts as the Uber rolls down Coxwell Street, then turns into the parking lot of EZ Storage, the only place I could find with a small unit on short notice. They offer a free moving truck to new customers but not to people with as little stuff as I have. Much like every other street, it looks like the zombie apocalypse has landed. Not a soul in sight.

I enter the facility through a side office attached to the big building where I assume my stuff will go. The first door bears a sign: Customer Service and Security Office; then another, more homemade one: Come in, we're open! A man greets me from behind a small teller-style window. He's wearing a nametag (Ed), rubber gloves and a suspicious expression. He looks to be a big guy: longish hair, very macho-looking. On the walls behind him are arranged rows of moving supplies — duct tape, rolls of shrink wrap, bungee cords and flattened cardboard boxes.

I wave and tell him I'm the one who called earlier. He nods, then lifts up the window and slides an envelope through the opening. He looks down at the envelope, then back at me. I move toward the counter to pick it up, and he practically flies backward about five feet — right, I forgot to replace my scarf. Still wordless, Ed points toward the elevator just down the hall. Inside the envelope is a card (Unit 2210) and a padlock with a key.

The Uber guy has since removed all my bags and boxes and unceremoniously piled them by the office building door. He's shifting back and forth, from one foot to the other. I guess the rest is up to me. I tap my card, tipping the guy a good five bucks less than if he'd at least hauled my stuff to the elevator.

***

It takes a few trips to get all my stuff up and into the unit. Even with everything I own in there, I'm surprised how much space there still is. Hell, I've seen smaller apartments! And the place is so new and clean.

Realizing suddenly how exhausted I am, I plop down onto a bag of clothes, whip out my phone and begin posting an SOS on my Insta and Snapchat. (Thank the goddess I got the LTE plan or I'd be fucked right now.) It's amazing how comfortable a pile of garbage bags full of clothes can be after a day like this…

Next thing I know, I'm waking up, still holding my phone. It's deadly quiet. It takes me a few seconds to remember where I am. And why. I've probably been asleep for a good three-plus hours, based on it being pitch black when I go into the hall and look out the window. It always gets dark so early in the winter. And it's deathly quiet. Has the guard left for the day? FML! I bolt back into the locker, hoping no one heard or saw me.

And there are some texts! First, my bestie, Nat. She would *love* to have me come stay with her, but her roommate isn't having it during quarantine. *Doesn't that bitch know I'm homeless?*

I'm SO sorry hun! texts Nat. *DW I'll keep working on her.* [Sad face with tears emoji]. *Now I'm officially worried about u. Keep txting me to check in, kk?*

I'm more worried now too. Nat has never not come through for me. The couple other friends I texted are no more able to help. Some of them are wondering if *they'll* even make the rent. One of them has an uncle who they think has the virus.

My stomach sinks. Then it occurs to me: If I try to leave now, where am I going to go? Is there another guard on night shift? It's eerily quiet but peaceful too. Is the place closed for the day? Even with the circumstances, I notice I'm actually calmer than I've been in days. I decide the best thing I can do is stay put, keep reaching out to more people and hope no one notices I've been here all night.

I retrieve my blanket from the pile, nestle in until the bags form a comfortable hollow for my body and start to Google *shelters near me*. About five results in, as worried and stressed as I am, I manage to drift off again.

When I next wake up, it's day, confirmed by the slat of light streaming in from the bottom of the roller door as I gently ease my fingers under it and slowly slide it up. What greets me reminds me of all those bad prison movies: a long hallway with a bunch of red roller doors like the one on my unit, with an exit to the stairs at either end. The fluorescent lights above create a candy-cane-like reflection on the concrete hall floor. Hunger stabs my lower gut. I'm jonesin' for a coffee and a smoke. And man, I wish I had a joint! Now I just have to get myself out of here without being seen. I can't even think about what I'm gonna do until I have a coffee.

I don't see any cameras in the ceiling. Probably in the stairwell. I hope they're not in the elevator too.

What day is it? Right, Thursday. The day after kick-Quinn-out-on-her-ass day. Will it be the same guard? Does it even matter? I remember when I came in yesterday, the elevator was at one side of the building. If I go out that way, he might see me leaving. So I walk to the stairwell at the other end of the hall. I'm just gonna have to risk being filmed rather than face that big guy again. He didn't look too happy yesterday.

I get there and — booyahhh! — it *is* an exit door! But fuck. Emergency exit only. Alarm will sound.

I decide to chance it. Squeezing my eyes tight, I blow through and sure enough, the damn alarm goes off. I keep running and duck around another building before anyone can see me.

***

At the Starbucks (Thank the goddess for Starbucks. Nothing ever makes them close!), I grab a steaming grande from the counter where it's placed by the masked barista, who then backs away three feet and motions to the debit machine. Right. I shoulda pulled my scarf up over my face. Still getting used to that.

The place is empty, all the tables pushed to one side and the chairs stacked up in two columns. They've put up a makeshift "velvet rope" of white tape on the floor to keep people lined up on one side. I pay, nodding gratefully, quickly grab a couple sugars and hit the ladies room to wash my hands (counting out the verses of "Happy Birthday" in my head, the ritual they'd been saying we should do for a few weeks now), then make my way out the side door where they've posted a handwritten sign: Customers please only exit here.

Sitting on a cold cement tree planter a few doors down, I sip my dark roast and tear into the slice of banana bread. Breakfast. Then the victory of having completed my coffee mission worn off, I light up a smoke and feel my stomach drop and throat tighten.

What now?

I have no job. No home. Everything is like a dystopian bizarro world. And it's still so freakin' cold out, even for April! And my phone is now at twelve percent. I shoulda dug out the charger last night. But where would I have plugged it in? Do storage units even *have* a place to plug in?

I don't want to tell my dad what's happening until I have a solution. He'll only feel bad because he really can't do anything.

"Fuck." I can feel my ass starting to numb from sitting on the cold cement. The sidewalk is practically empty. I observe two people across the street coming from opposite directions swerve to avoid walking near each other. One of them does an about-face before crossing to the other side, not needing to look both ways, there's only one car going by every thirty seconds or so. And this is freakin' Queen Street.

My mind jolts back to my pathetic situation. I have to go back to the unit to get my charger and a few supplies, to take to whatever shelter or church will have me. I shoulda done that before coming out. That alarm might have fucked me for my storage space ... or worse.

I get back to EZ Storage and, fortunately, whatshisname (Ted?) is not at his wicket. Phew! Now I just gotta get back to the locker for my charger. And find a place to plug in — I'm at four freakin' percent now! Oh, and start packing a bag with my most-needed supplies.

Who knows where I'm gonna be tonight?

I grab my big backpack, my favourite one that I used to take to marches and festival road trips. It's dotted with rainbow flags and slogan buttons and my favourite pink triangle patch; stamps on my Pride passport.

No one knows where I am.

Wait ... someone does. The door rolls up and there stands that bulky guard. Ed. (I was close!)

"You're back."

"Ummm ... yeah, I forgot a few things yesterday."

"No, I mean after leaving this morning — the alarm goes off if someone uses those doors during closing time. Then the camera caught you exiting. And there's the access log — nothing on there about your leaving last night."

His eyes narrow and he leans forward, though still keeping a good five feet of distance between us. "Do you know how much trouble I'll be in if the owners knew I let someone stay here? This isn't the States, you know."

I feel hot tears welling up as I start to blab. "I am so sorry, sir, um ... Ed ... so I got kicked outta my place yesterday because of the virus and haven't been able to find a place to stay ... I was texting a bunch of people last night and I guess with all the stress I fell asleep, and now my phone is dying, and my mom is dead, my dad in a whole other country..." I start to sob and hyperventilate. Embarrassed, I hold my bag up to shield my face. This guy doesn't care about my problems. And from the looks of him, he likely doesn't take well to such displays of weakness.

But when I lower my bag, his face has softened. "Wait. You're homeless?"

I can only nod, my face a mess of tears, sweat and snot.

He continues in a calmer tone. "Listen. How do you feel about cleaning?"

I don't understand, so decide it's wiser to keep my mouth shut.

"I don't just work here. I live here too," he says. "Upstairs. The owners want me to start going around and cleaning all the door handles. And the outside entrance, loading dock doors, bathrooms, elevator buttons ... anything anyone touches. They won't just hire someone else, tight-asses. Nice people, but, typical Jews, they really do hold on to their money." He folded his arms in front of him.

"It's gonna be pretty hard for me to do that, do my normal rounds and keep an eye on the cameras. And I'm gonna need to be more alert, especially if there are more people like you out there at loose ends — maybe some who aren't as ... innocent." I blink at him, unsure where he's going with this. "So here's the deal. I can let you stay here while you're renting the unit. In exchange, you do the cleaning. You have to get a mask and gloves. We have the cleaning stuff. The bosses just won't know it's you doing the cleaning."

Ed is on a roll. I'm gobsmacked but also feel my gut start to unclench.

"Now listen carefully: There'll be rules you have to follow to make sure no one knows you're staying here. To start with, you'll have to use the bathroom to charge your phone. You probably noticed there's no power in your unit. I'll write everything else down for you."

Then he does the next last thing I expect. He takes out his phone and scrolls for half a minute, then holds it up facing me. Even from two metres I can make out what's in the photo: It's a younger Ed in a black muscle shirt, shyly squinting toward the camera. Next to him is a guy wearing denim cut-offs, a white tank top and several gold chains. His right arm is draped over Ed's shoulder, the other high above his head, brandishing a rainbow flag.

I feel the urge to rush in and hug my new ally, but he stiffens as I start toward him. "Hey! We still have to keep our distance."

I wipe my face with my sleeve and repress the urge to at least shake his hand or give him a fist bump. "Thank you. You don't know what you've done here. I was getting so scared and—"

He holds up his right hand, then grins, now more like the Ed in the picture. "Just keep a low profile and we're all good. So hey, you can relax. Charge your phone. Settle in. I'll see you at my office tomorrow morning at eight thirty sharp." He grins again. "You *do* have an alarm in that phone, right?"

EZ Storage Ex-Bouncer Employee Eduardo

Main office and upstairs apartment: 200'×300'
This bachelor apartment above the main office holds just enough furniture for one person.

Eduardo Ruiz had been an orphan almost seventeen years now.

So, when he spied the rainbow triangle on Quinn's backpack and she told him about her mom being dead, he quickly put together that they were more the same than they were different. And that's when he'd decided to go against policy and let her stay in her unit.

When Quinn said she had no place to go, and with everything else she'd told him — although some of it was hard to decipher as she cried and hyperventilated — Ed's usually untappable heart melted. No, not in that way.

More like how you would feel toward your kid sister if you saw her upset and were overcome with the need to protect her.

And it wasn't completely unselfish, letting her stay in her unit. It would really help cover *his* ass too, because there was no way he was going to be able to keep cleaning and sanitizing the unit while still keeping guard. Fucking coronavirus — where the hell'd that come from? Just when he was feeling like he finally knew every corner of EZ Storage.

Hell, if that skinny chick got in and out with me not knowing, imagine what'll happen if more people who are sneakier and more dangerous than her start showing up here. He made a mental note to talk to her about texting him if she noticed any suspicious-looking people as she made her way along each of the floors.

And so, *gracias a Dios*, now he wouldn't have to worry about falling behind. With all the crap jobs he'd had, he'd never had to be a cleaner. He was a security guard! He wasn't about to start being the fuckin' cleaning lady!

He probably had a good ten or more years on Quinn. So she could cover more ground more quickly, likely having the energy to clean the door handles of a good hundred or more units a day, while he did a rotation of the four bathrooms and elevator buttons. They would just have to keep their distance from each other if their paths met in the course of the day.

Before this virus *de mierda*, when had this level of cleanliness ever been so important in a freakin' storage place? EZ Storage was still only ten years old, so it was in pretty good shape. Not like the ones on *Storage Wars*, where they'd sometimes even find people living, a lot of them hillbilly trash in the middle of buttfuck nowhere.

Ed may not have finished high school, but he'd secured a major perk of the job: a full apartment in the attached office building. Unlike poor Quinn, he didn't have to live *in* a storage locker.

Dios mío, all he would need would be that Elliot guy (or was it Walter?) with the freaking eBay store showing up and trying to make some kind of deal with him to let him sleep there. No thanks; that guy gave off a weird vibe. Sneaky, guilty about something. Plus he'd probably leave trash outside the door in the morning. He didn't look like the type who would take out his own garbage.

And anyway, most of the time he knew who was trying to hang around past closing time. In his walkarounds, he could see whose units had their padlocks closed — those who didn't usually had the doors at least partially rolled up. And there were automated access logs connected to the cameras.

Oh shit. He forgot to tell her that once every couple of weeks the owners came. *She better get her ass back to her unit, or better yet, just not be here.* They'd work out a system where he would text if he knew they were coming. They'd both be fucked if anyone found out about their arrangement. And Ed had been pretty lonely already in his new apartment, even before everybody else had to be stuck at home. It had been only a fucking month of this. At least before living here, he could go out and stay out for hours, getting what he needed and then holing up for the night in his apartment. And he didn't have to cover his face to do it or wash his hands every time he came and went.

Just a few short months before, he could meet his boys and go grab a few, watch the wave of sweaty young gay boys start to fill the dance floor, some eyeing each other furtively, and escape to the memories of his cruising days, about ten years earlier, a few months after he'd landed from Central America. Lately, he felt doomed to go a long stretch alone. Even before the pandemic, he'd noticed his Grindr responses dwindling steadily. And the ones who'd thrown him Likes were often the same dudes he'd swiped left on before, and who had now shown up with another profile name. *I may not have more than Grade 10, but do they think I'm that stupid?*

He was jolted back to the present when he heard a knock on the office window. It was that chick, Nina. She had a purple sequined scarf tied over her face. She was there to extend her contract by another couple of months; she said this from partway down the hall. No one even spoke to him from just outside the window now, let alone came into his office.

She'd backed up about eight feet, had him drop the paperwork on the floor of the hallway that connected his office to the main building, then come back up once he'd gone back into his office, sprayed some orange liquid onto her hands, signed the paper, put it back down and sprayed her hands again. Finally, she sashayed away in the other direction toward the elevator, waving him off with her right hand, not even turning around again.

When Nina had last been at the storage unit — what was it, six or seven months ago? — he'd been in the connecting hallway, about to do his afternoon rounds. She'd had a plastic dry-cleaning bag over her shoulder that covered a pile of glittery, skimpy dresses. If he were attracted to women, he might've wanted to see his girlfriend in that little blue number!

Perhaps detecting his fixation on her, she looked back his way after pressing the elevator button. "Could you see me wearing these?" Then, barely waiting for an answer, she continued, "Nah, these I'm selling. They were from one of the girls that didn't even last the week. Not my style at all … and I'm at least a size smaller than her." She jutted one hip out flirtatiously, resting her free hand on the other. "Might you have a special lady who's looking to buy some sexy high-end dresses?"

Ed chuckled and shook his head without lifting it, which seemed to satisfy Nina, whose elevator had arrived. She must've figured out by now that she wasn't his type. And anyway, he knew that even if he'd been interested, with that one, he'd need to pay for it. Plus he'd been turned off by the way she'd made a point of trying to guess his race the first time they'd met.

"Hey, you're Native, right?"

"No, I came from Central America." He didn't usually name the actual country, because then it would mean he might have to explain that no, his father did not die in heroic defence of their country against Martí's guerrillas nor his mother of grief for her husband. No, their demise had been far less heroic.

The food packaging plant they'd worked in had exploded and then burned to the ground. They'd waited twelve years to get the same shift at the factory. Some reward for their years of hard labour.

Ed had always wondered how they'd even been able to conceive him, with one overlapping hour being the only time they'd see each other over a sixteen-hour period each day, often during weekends too. They must have had to give up a lot of sleep to spend any time together. And as a result, he'd been mostly raised by his *abuelita* until he was about nine.

When Nina had cocked her head and threw him a confused expression — a look she'd likely practised, to get her those extra clients who liked the dumb ones — Ed asked himself whether he should bother explaining that, no, he was not a Native Indian of any country. His father had Indigenous lineage, but his family never mentioned it, likely since it wouldn't help further their desired ability to blend in.

So Ed felt no more affinity with Indigenous Canadians than he did with Indigenous Peoples from back home. He was thankful for his good hair, thick and black, which he wore long because he was a rocker who loved him some Zeppelin, Sabbath and Rush.

Back to the little girl with the nose ring ... Quinn. It was the rainbow triangle that turned him. He realized he had at times felt as completely alone as she probably did. And he also knew it would be harder for someone like them to find a place to crash. He was going to have to make damn sure that she was not here when the owners dropped by. One of them was really nice, the other a complete bastard.

Even before he'd moved in here, it had been pretty grey and boxed-in for Ed — after Joaquín moved out. In exchange for taking his heart, he'd left Ed with twice the rent, which in Toronto would be impossible to pay after the first six weeks or so, with the little he had put aside. And he wasn't getting no roommate!

From the time he started last August, his bosses had been asking him to consider a move-in position. The apartment above the office had a shower, a dishwasher and everything. Suddenly having a rent-free place and a full-time salary on top, how could he say no? His current situation made it a no-brainer, so he handed in his notice at the pricey apartment and settled in thirty days later.

But now it was starting to sink in that no one really knew how much worse this covid thing was going to get. Would more people lose their jobs? And what was that going to mean for business? Would some people stop paying? Would more people start coming? Would someone start something if Ed had to get them to leave? (Not to mention, he didn't want to get close enough to anyone that he might catch this fuckin' thing. But he did have a job to do if it came to that.) You had to be prepared for these situations.

The other day he thought he'd seen the effects of the virus in the face of one of the least-threatening customers, that guy who always brought the exact same bins. Tony ... no, Toby. Right. He had a tiny unit, and Ed had only ever seen him a couple times, always with those same grey plastic containers he would roll in on a dolly from the loading dock. Other than when he'd come to sign the contract, he'd put off a vibe of being unapproachable, lowering his head behind the piled boxes, looking down at his feet.

"Hey there, Tobe, good to see you're wearing a mask. You know, a lot of other customers aren't as careful as you." Ed felt like he wanted to say something to cheer the guy up.

The man looked up with his usual air of being caught off guard. "Oh ... yeah. Well my girlfriend is really nervous about us getting sick..." He looked back down, but not before Ed perceived the fear in his eyes.

Realizing he had called the guy "Tobe," Ed clammed up and put his head down to look at his iPad. He'd probably embarrassed this pale distracted soul. He heard the man's footsteps getting fainter and only then looked back up. He really did have to keep his guard up.

He learned all about keeping up his guard years before getting his first few security gigs as a bouncer at one of the straightest bars he'd ever set foot in. He'd found it refreshingly easy to stay focused on his work, mostly hanging out by the door and deciding who in line would get in, and almost no one would dare challenge him, at six foot four and ripped, evident from his black muscle shirt. But there was the odd time...

As a younger kid, he'd taken karate for a handful of years, finding that it made him stand another inch taller by the time he got his black belt. So even though he'd only gotten up to Grade 10 in regular school, he credited his time at the dojo with giving him the confidence and ability to get the bouncer job.

What was funnier to Ed was that they probably hired him because of how straight he looked. And though at times there were some guys worth a second look in the lineups, the fact that they were often already half-drunk and hanging all over the girls they had in tow made any attraction melt away like candle wax.

Around that time someone had told him he looked like the guy that played the Hulk in the Avengers movies. He was pretty big but not enough to pick the Bear category in Grindr. And his hair was a lot longer than that guy's. Though still, it may have been this resemblance that had gotten him the job at My Penthouse. Ed thought the reason they kept him seven years was that he never hit on the girls at the door. (Their previous bouncer had been ejected after accepting *special favours* in return for front-of-the-line status.) They wanted a straight guy to intimidate the other straight guys but not so straight that he'd hit on their girlfriends.

But that had been a whole other time, when people had let their guard down more than ... Holy shit, he just realized — if he had that job now, he'd be unemployed! No one could even go into a fuckin' Tim Hortons now, let alone a bar. Maybe he should be thankful being all holed up in this echoey place full of O.P.P. (other people's problems) recalling that Naughty By Nature classic — because people usually got units here after having some kind of problem, right?

Like divorces. So many of the clients ended up here after splitting with someone. Someone goes away and doesn't come back; someone downsizes or can't get over their past; so they keep all this shit to remind them of when everything seemed okay.

He thought about that lady whose kids were always calling, always irritated, asking for the owners to give them a few more days to pay her bill. Barely anyone came to attend to her shit, including her. Eventually, they came and got her stuff out and ended the contract, settling the $765 debt she'd managed to rack up only three months after her brother had paid an even higher bill.

But they didn't care enough about the shit to actually keep it in their homes, where other people could see. *Maybe now that everyone's stuck at home, some of these people will start wanting their old shit back.* One of the ones Ed knew would be among the first to come for his shit was that short guy with the '70s rock-and-roll hair and the red face. He showed up every so often to "check on" his stuff. The little dude looked like a good guy, often had a pair of skates slung over his shoulder. Sometimes an older couple would come by to put things in the same unit. Kind of like that sad old lady and her kids — it seemed like more than one family member had a stake in the stuff at EZ Storage.

Even before seeing that they'd visited the same unit, Ed put it together that they were from the same family when, on meeting the older couple and having run into their small red-faced son only a week before, he thought they looked familiar.

Familiar. Like he knew much about that. Having emigrated and gotten his PR card mere weeks before his first Canadian boyfriend. Feeling like a foreigner, even sometimes now, he felt his grip on *familiar* was pretty fragile.

But thank God he'd gotten the fuck outta El Salvador and hooked up with that tasty-looking daddy. Ed had already started his bouncer gig and moved down to the east end of the city, not far from the lake. It was so much nicer being there than by a mass of concrete connected by underground malls at the top of the subway line.

EZ had been part of his 'hood before he started working and eventually living there. And it had been a pretty easy gig to get, once he told them his full name, that is.

"Eduardo Ruiz."

"The one that…"

"Yes. We've met before."

That previous meeting occurred when he'd helped get a situation under control a few weeks before he'd applied for the job. It involved that sad lady with the kids who were fighting all the time about paying for her unit and were always calling to make more excuses for why she hadn't paid. He'd since learned they'd managed to save her stuff from being sold off more than once over the years. He thought the owners felt sorry for her. They were Jewish too, and didn't those people take care of their own?

That first time he saw her, she was in front of the office with a younger man standing over her, yelling. The man wasn't much taller than she was and had the same curly hair, but without the grey. His finger was right in her face, as he jabbed at the air to accentuate every point. Along with the resemblance, he looked about thirty-eight, which would make him the right age to be her son, since the woman looked to be about sixty.

The woman looked afraid but also somehow indignant, like she might be the type that would push people's buttons. But mostly, Ed felt sorry for her. He didn't care who she was. He couldn't just go by and let that shit happen. And not having his own mother, he was very sensitive to watching anybody mistreat theirs.

Ed had gotten off his bike and started toward them. Things had gotten loud — people walking by were staring, a passing couple was whispering.

"Do you need help?" Ed said to the woman.

The son turned to look up at him, finger paused midair. "Excuse me, but this is a private family matter." The man's eyes were narrowing further with each word.

The woman looked up at Ed too. Her eyes looked like they were covered in Vaseline. "This is my son. He and I are just having a conversation." She looked like she only half-believed what she had said.

"Okay," said Ed, "but it doesn't look like he's just talking to you, with all due respect, ma'am."

At this point, another man came out of the office. He would turn out to be Ike Hurwitz, one of the two owners, and the nicer of the two.

"What is going *on* here?"

"This man is mad at his mother," said Ed. "That's as much as I got."

The son then turned on the new arrival, who he bested in height by about an inch. "This is a private conversation, Ike. Do you mind?" Son of the Year's teeth were gritted, a foam of spittle forming at the corner of his snarl.

Ike was a really small guy. He didn't look big or young enough to be able to contain Sonny Boy's rage.

"I just think you're talking pretty mean to your mom there," Ed piped up.

"It's okay," said Ike. "These are customers here. Our families know each other."

Ed still wasn't convinced little Ike was going to be able to handle this. But satisfied that the owner's arrival had at least lowered the heat on the argument, he said,

"Okay, but if this gets worse and you need a witness or some backup, here's my card."

Ed had the cards made before he'd taken the job at the airport and carried them anywhere he went.

Eduardo Gutierrez Ruiz.
Security. Small machine maintenance.
Handyman. Available for hire.
(647) 555-0900. BigEd54731@hotmail.com.

He then hopped back on his bike but not without making a point of leaning on the handlebars so that his biceps were in full view of Sonny Boy, who, no longer looking so confident, stormed off toward a black convertible, shaking his head the whole way.

"Stephen isn't usually this rude," said the mother, brightening a bit more with each step her son took in the opposite direction.

The next morning, Ed had gotten a call from Ike, thanking him for intervening. At that time neither he nor Ike knew that Sonny Boy would soon become a customer of EZ Storage, because a few months later, his wife would leave him (a fact that didn't surprise Ed). He'd recently found out about what happened to Stephen — or Steve, as he preferred — from the man himself, who seemed to have forgotten all about their standoff the first time they'd met.

And Ed didn't yet know that Ike would end up being his boss before long. But now Ed knew he'd been given a chance. And he was hoping he could help another scared gay orphaned soul find their own fate, with a place to curl up safely every night. His thoughts turned again to the possibility that, like that helpless young girlie, other people would want to live with their shit now. Could there be a side hustle in this? He immediately pushed the thought out of his head. *Fuck, now don't start thinking about how to make more money from the bosses. Compared to some other guys, I'm doing good!*

Take the guy his ex was living with, Andre. He was probably gonna lose his bar. Even though Ed would have rather seen him dead when he first learned of Andre's involvement with Joaquín, Ed didn't hold any ill will toward the guy anymore. After all, Ed was a man of honour! Even the person his ex cheated on him with shouldn't have to lose his livelihood all because of a virus. *We know so little about how dangerous this thing is or whether it's only going to last a short time.* Yet people were losing their freakin' minds — and their businesses — at a pace that bewildered Ed.

To add to things, Ed even held a secret admiration for the one who would start keeping Joaquín warm — at least his ex had found someone with a bit more brains than he had; someone who could satisfy his craving for the finer things. La dolce vita.

During better times, Ed would muss Joaquín's hair affectionately, teasing him about how "snotty and snobby" he could be. "Gimme some Zeppelin and a cold one, maybe a patio on Queen, like at the Black Bull. And

I'm good," Ed would say, usually with his voice raised over the pulsating thump of electronic music that attached itself to the entourage his ex ferried everywhere he went. Not that he hadn't had experiences of his own — after all, he was an orphan from Central America — so you could for sure say he'd seen some shit. And not that there weren't other things that bothered him about Joaquín. A lot of that over-the-top queerness tried his patience. If he hadn't loved his ex so much, he'd have stayed away from someone so comfortably out.

For his part, Ed preferred being able to choose the moment when someone would learn he was gay; so at times he felt like being with someone who called half of their male friends "she" and "honey" had outed him without his consent. It was also why he was not at all a fan of PDA. And Joaquín had always introduced him as "Eduardo" when they went out. He would always gently correct him: "It's Ed." And in turn he called Joaquín "Jack," especially in public, even though everyone else called him by his given name. Ed felt that would just draw more attention to their minority status. As if they didn't already face enough challenges as a Hispanic same-sex couple, with the culture of machismo they'd grown up in!

One night last year, not long before Joaquín moved out, they had one of their countless conversations about the differences in how they looked at things. "But don't you ever think there's a whole world out there of experiences and places, man?" Joaquín had parked at the top of a hill and they'd walked to a grassy area overlooking a cliff. The Scarborough Bluffs, Ed thought it was called. The man Joaquín would later leave Ed for owned a houseboat in the marina there, something Ed would find ironic later on, given that he would end up living by the lake himself. "I mean, this lake. It's beautiful and all," Joaquín continued, "but there are so many oceans I long to swim in, go jet skiing, wakeboarding … new, amazing places to check out, just waiting for us!"

Yeah, easy for him to say. He's set for life. The rest of us have to work for a living.

"Don't you ever want to go somewhere besides El Salvador and Toronto?"

Ed had paused then. He liked to think before answering a question about something important. And coming from his Jack, it was *all* important. "You know, I don't really feel the need to go all over the place to feel I've experienced enough. I'm pretty satisfied with what I have right here." He tightened his grip on Joaquín's triceps while saying this. "And you know I have a good imagination. I can go anywhere in my imagination." (His Jack knew *that* was right, unless he'd been faking his appreciation of the many ways Ed had demonstrated his imagination with his body.)

"I don't need to be able to post on my Insta about all the places I go," he'd continued. "I'm happy with where I am already. Right now, here. I've worked hard to get where I am. And I'll keep working hard." He'd tipped his beer bottle up. "Far as I'm concerned, I came out ahead."

But even though he felt trusting enough of Joaquín to bare his soul to him that night, Ed already had a feeling then and there that their relationship would probably not last much longer. He'd learned all about living in the moment from his sensei. The whole Zen thing. That — and what he'd learned (the hard way; Sensei Louis didn't hold back) about not telegraphing his movements while fighting — had been the most important lessons he'd learned at the dojo as a boy.

Looking back now, he was reminded of how he'd already had three strikes against him that he'd managed to overcome: He was an orphaned only child; he was an immigrant who hadn't finished high school; and he was gay. The fact that he'd gotten a place to live along with a legit job? He knew not to expect more than the insane amount of good luck he'd already had. He wasn't gonna go and jinx it.

And thank fuck he'd not met someone from the States or maybe he'd be living there now. "Imagine having Trump making decisions for us," he said. *Then again, I probably wouldn't have even been able to live there. No doubt they'd lump me in with the Mexicans and throw me back over The Wall.*

And now there's this thing that no one in the world seems to be able to escape. A pandemic. People were losing their shit and their jobs left and right. The news out of New York changed by the hour. And now he'd decided to risk his job to have a homeless little lesbian help him out at work.

The last time Ed had seen that kind of terror in a woman's eyes, it'd been the night he'd almost knocked over that little woman who'd crashed into him in the hall, her eyes confused and afraid at the same time. She'd stopped, flustered, silent, then darted away like a rabbit to the stairwell at the end of the hall. (He wondered why she didn't just take the elevator.)

He'd turned and seen a guy at the other end of the hall, at the doorway of a unit, door rolled up, what looked like a women's nightgown at his feet and wearing a similar shocked — but also ashamed — expression. She'd been so tiny and unassuming, he'd been surprised at how hard she'd crashed into him and how quickly she'd resumed her frantic pace. He'd never seen this woman but had definitely seen the guy before. It was that guy Elliott — dammit, no, *Walter* — he'd been thinking about earlier.

Ed had always figured the guy was running an eBay store or something. The few times he'd crossed Ed's path, he was carrying hangers of women's clothing. Ed wasn't going to bother digging for more info about the guy's business in the unit; he was always polite as he came and went, and it wasn't like he was moving boxes of merchandise into the loading dock — stuff of his only ever seemed to *leave* the building.

He thought again about Quinn, now wondering why he hadn't just told her to take her shit and go. After all, he had a feeling things were going to get worse before they got better.

But that was just it. He figured that if he did something nice for someone, something he wouldn't normally ever do, maybe good fortune would stay with him. Hopefully he'd be able to come through whatever was about to happen without losing any of what he had now. The things he'd worked so hard to get.

'Cause married or divorced, old or young, gay or straight, he had a feeling some bigger shit than this was waiting just around the corner, for *all* of them.

Acknowledgments

Lots of people deserve props for helping me finish and publish this book.

First off, a few readers helped me with those first couple stories that led to my continuing with the rest. My kick-ass friend, neighbour and karaoke partner, Michelle Byrn, added her sharp eye to those early versions, as did my bright and beautiful daughter, Kyra Black; sharp-eyed mom, Donna Croke; and cherished lifelong friend, Raquel Grave. Thank you, Marian Reich, my karate and yoga co-conspirator, for your great suggestion about how to create an intriguing connection between a few of the characters via the lost-then-found hockey card. And thanks again to Michelle for giving the whole thing a last, objective pass and sharpening the prose up further so I could confidently meet my deadline.

I am grateful as well for the support of the team of utter pros at Iguana Books: president Greg Ioannou (who also happens to be my dear, long-time friend and colleague), editor Paula Chiarcos, proofreader Holly Warren and managing editor Cheryl Hawley. Thank you all for lending the manuscript your magic to help shape the narrative and give it greater credibility — and for being so easy to work with! I knew I was in good hands at every step of the process.

Paula, your suggestion to run certain characters by people who more closely share their experience was golden. Simon Arès, Jesse Gough, Raquel Grave and Enrique J Sáenz all devoted time to help me make 'tit Mo and his family, Quinn and Ed truer to life, since they weren't people I could relate to first-hand.

Then there's artist and designer Sam Hlaing, who created the cover. After several years of exchanges over the cubicle wall, it was wonderful to connect again for purely creative means! I appreciate your receptivity to my many requests for revisions.

Lastly, I must acknowledge Tami Tester, the helpful and friendly employee of a local storage facility who showed me around and answered all of my questions. This research kept me honest in setting the scene and giving it authenticity. She didn't know at the time that the questions were research for the book. But now, on receiving a signed copy with this acknowledgment, she will.

About the Author

Michelle Black is a writer and editor who for many years ran a plain language consulting business. Having helped others improve their writing voice for decades, Michelle is exploring her own voice as a creative writer. A karate black belt who speaks three languages, Michelle can identify birds and garden flowers, and is passionate about music, especially the artist Prince.

Michelle grew up in Toronto, where she still resides with her two teenagers. She has never rented a storage unit.

CPSIA information can be obtained
at www.ICGtesting.com
Printed in the USA
BVHW052106221122
652538BV00001B/6

9 781771 805841